D0069408

the hunger

To my grandmother,
Josephine Dennis.

the hunger

the hunger
the hunger

marsha forchuk skrypuch

THE DUNDURN GROUP
A BOARDWALK BOOK
TORONTO

Boardwalk Books
A Member of the Dundurn Group

Publisher: J. Kirk Howard
Editor: Marc Côté
Copyeditor: Barry Jowett
Design: Jennifer Scott
Printer: Transcontinental Printing, Inc.

Canadian Cataloguing in Publication Data
Skrypuch, Marsha Forchuk, 1954–
The hunger

ISBN 1-895681-16-2
I. Title.
PS8587.K79H83 1999 jC813'.54 C99-932271-0
PZ7.S57Hu 1999

3 4 5 09 08 07 06 05

Canada Council
for the Arts

Canada

We acknowledge the support of the **Canada Council for the Arts** and the **Ontario Arts Council** for our publishing program. We also acknowledge the financial support of the **Government of Canada** through the **Book Publishing Industry Development Program** and **The Association for the Export of Canadian Books**, and the **Government of Ontario** through the **Ontario Book Publishers Tax Credit program**, and the **Ontario Media Development Corporation**.

Care has been taken to trace the ownership of copyright material used in this book. The author and the publisher welcome any information enabling them to rectify any references or credits in subsequent editions.

J. Kirk Howard, President

Printed and bound in Canada.
www.dundurn.com

Dundurn Press
3 Church Street, Suite 500
Toronto, Ontario, Canada
M5E 1M2

Gazelle Book Services Limited
White Cross Mills
Hightown, Lancaster, England
LA1 4X5

Dundurn Press
2250 Military Road
Tonawanda, NY
U.S.A. 14150

Acknowledgements

My first thank you goes to Carl Georgian, whose own father, Kevork Kevorkian (George Georgian) was a Georgetown Boy. Carl generously shared with me the story of his father's arrival to Canada, and it is that story that originally inspired me to write this one. I would also like to thank the late Aram Aivazian, a survivor of the massacres and an historian in his own right. Aram generously shared with me his vast collection of rare books and also his vast memory of horrific historical events.

The reality of Paula's anorexia would not have been possible without insight from my dear friend, Heather Blakely — a survivor. I would also like to thank the counsellors who allowed me to interview them. They remain nameless at their own request. Doctors Leslie Leach, David Thompson, and Derek Dabreo assisted enormously in a myriad of medical details. My husband, Dr. Orest Skrypuch, helped me in all things computer-related, and also in many things medical. My son, Neil, was my *Civ II* coach. Martina Boone, as always, deserves many thanks for her fine writerly eye.

At The Dundurn Group, I would like to thank Barry Jowett, for it was he who first chose my manuscript amidst the many on his desk and recommended it for further consideration.

A sincere thank you to Marc Côté, associate publisher at Dundurn. Marc's precise editorial insight pushed me to make *The Hunger* the best novel that it could be.

And a special thank you to my agent, Dean Cooke, for his faith and encouragement.

the hunger

Thursday, June 24

"Okay girls, let's not dawdle."

Miss Brenman was small and lean and could have been a ballerina. She seemed to take great pleasure in showing off her figure for the benefit of the group of self-conscious girls who made up the bulk of her Grade 9 gym class. "Get into your groups," she called out. "Group A, line up at the balance beam. Janet, you can be the spotter."

Paula towered over the other four girls in group A. With her black hair hanging in her face, she walked over to the beam and jockeyed for last place in the short line. Janet, who was lithe and supple like Miss Brenman, smirked at the other girls. "Let's start with a simple knee scale."

Simple? There was nothing simple about any of the movements as far as Paula was concerned. Her ever-increasing height made her feel so awkward. It was as if as soon as she got used to her new centre of gravity, it moved! She looked around the room at the other groups and watched as one of her classmates somersaulted gracefully over the pommel horse. Paula could have performed that somersault twelve months ago. A group of girls cheered as one of their classmates did cartwheels halfway across the gym floor. It's so effortless for them! Why did she have to be so big and awkward?

In her own group, Suzy Nguyen was chosen to go first. Paula watched the tiny Vietnamese girl approach the bar with trepidation. Suzie was slim, but she had short legs and no sense of balance. Miraculously, she did her knee scale without falling.

Janet smiled broadly and helped the trembling girl down. "That was just fine, Sooz!"

Suzy smiled weakly at Janet, but Paula noticed that she was fighting back tears.

"Your turn!" The smiling Janet pointed at Paula.

Paula stepped up to the narrow beam of polished wood and gripped it with both hands. Placing her foot onto the block of wood that the girls used as a step, Paula gingerly hoisted herself up until her knees touched the top edge of the cold expanse of wood. She turned so that her body was lined in the same direction as the bar. Her knees were tight together on the bar, but even so, they felt too big for it. She had a queasy feeling in the pit of her stomach as she wobbled back and forth, hands gripped tightly on the bar and knees feeling like they were about to slip off.

"Hurry up, Paul," admonished Janet, hands on hips. "We don't have all day."

Paula took a deep breath and tried to quell the thumping of her heart. Janet's words only increased the tension she was feeling. Slowly, slowly, she straightened out one knee and began to draw her long leg out in her best approximation of the "simple" knee scale. Her arms were trembling and her knees ached, but miraculously, she was perfectly balanced! This was the first time she had been able to do a knee scale since her growth spurt. Her heart swelled with pride and, for a nanosecond, she forgot how uncomfortable she was.

"Stretch it out a bit more, Paul, you're almost there," said Janet dispassionately.

Almost there?? Paula couldn't believe it. Didn't Janet realize how difficult it was for her to be doing this at all? "I can't stretch it out any more," said Paula, her brief feeling of pride squelched.

"Sure you can." Janet walked over to Paula and roughly adjusted Paula's leg, pulling it into the proper position.

In a flash, Paula crashed to the ground. Knives of pain radiated through the small of her back. The pain she could handle. Far worse was Janet laughing at her.

"Paul, it's a good thing you've got so much padding, otherwise you could've hurt yourself!"

Paula curled into a fetal position and hid her face in her knees. All around her, girls tittered nervously. Paula covered her ears with her hands, but she couldn't block out the sound.

Canada Day, Wednesday July 1

Paula snuggled deep in her comforter, half asleep and half awake, savouring the opportunity to sleep in. She had written her final exams right up until the 26th, and then spent the last two mornings babysitting Sara and Tara, the twins next door.

"Paula, the day's wasting away. Get up!"

Her father's voice jolted her out of her reveries. Paula's first inclination was to snuggle even deeper into the warmth of her comforter, and pretend that she was asleep, but she knew it would do no good. Her father had the day off, and her father wanted to take a nice long run, with his daughter.

She pulled the covers away from her face and squinted up at the figure in the hallway. Erik Romaniuk was already dressed in a T-shirt and well-used pair of jogging shorts that were far too short for a man of his age. Or most men his age.

"I'll meet you downstairs in five," he said.

Paula could hear him walk down the hallway to her brother, Erik's room. Paula smiled to herself. Fat chance that Erik would go running with them.

Paula got out of bed and opened her drawer, rooting through to find a pair of shorts that she could wear that wouldn't ride up on her thighs as she ran. She decided on a pair of black form-fitting bicycle shorts. She threw on an oversized T-shirt and headed down the stairs.

As expected, Erik was not in sight. Mr. Romaniuk answered Paula's unasked question as he followed her gaze to her brother's empty chair. "At least I've got one athletic kid."

Paula gulped down some orange juice and then followed her father out the door. They did their warm-up stretches on the front steps. "This run will do us some good," he said

Paula felt her face flush hot.

Monday, July 6

"Come on, Mandy! It's a two-for-one sale. Besides, I really don't want to join an aerobics class by myself." The ad taped to the door of the Rotary Recreation Centre was a "students only" special. Paula had walked over to Mandy's house after babysitting, and the two were on their way to the mall when they passed by the fitness centre and decided to check it out.

"I wonder why it's so cheap?" Mandy tried to peer in through the tinted window.

"Maybe their regulars are off on summer holidays," offered Paula. "Who cares? As long as it's cheap." Paula pushed open the door, and both girls walked in.

They were greeted with a cheerful smile by a slim blonde sitting at the reception desk. The badge pinned to the front of her cropped T-shirt identified her as Debi Black, trainer. "Would you two like a tour?" she asked.

They followed her up the stairs and Paula couldn't help but notice that Debi looked fantastic in her spandex thigh-length shorts.

The top of the stairs opened up onto a running track and weight room with a full length mirror covering one wall. "Are you interested in weight training, or aerobics classes?" asked the woman.

"The classes," said Mandy.

"This is where they're held." Debi directed them into a room with floor-to-ceiling windows on one side, and floor-to-ceiling mirrors on another. There was a stack of mats in the corner and a ghetto blaster on a table in the front. A faint smell of sweat and baby powder hung in the air.

"I've got to get back downstairs," said Debi. "Take your time and look around. When you come back down, we can go over the class times."

Once Debi left, Paula and Mandy stood side by side in front of the aerobics mirror. Paula looked at the reflection of her best friend and stifled a sigh of jealousy. Mandy's thick red-gold hair rippled in waves down her back, accentuating her tiny waist.

Paula walked out of the aerobics room and back through the weight room to head down the stairs. She noticed a lithe woman doing bicep curls on an incline bench. Like Mandy, the woman was small.

The Hunger

Tuesday, September 7

Paula hugged her textbooks to her chest as she walked down the school hallway to her first class of the year. She noted through the corner of her eye that the guys looked at her appreciatively. The modest weight loss that she had achieved over the summer had made a difference. She suppressed a grin as she passed Miss Brenman, whose mouth had opened in a tiny O as she walked by.

Paula had a feeling that this was going to be her year. After so much trying, she was finally on her way to almost complete perfection. Her Grade 9 final report card couldn't have been better; now she looked slim and athletic — she was the envy of all.

She sat down in one of the desks in the front row and opened her binder. She heard a ripple of whispers behind her and she knew she was being talked about. A smile played on the corners of her lips.

Mr. Brown walked in moments before the bell rang. He took out a sheaf of papers from his briefcase and began to pass out one to each student. "This is the course outline for Enriched Multicultural History 201," he said as he walked through the aisles, passing out sheets. "You'll notice that 20 percent of your mark is based on class participation; 20 percent on tests; and 25 percent on your final exam. The rest of your mark will be based on your year-long project."

As he finished the last phrase, a groan rose from the class. The big problem with the enriched classes was that there was always some huge year-long assignment.

Paula didn't groan. While other students would put off their big assignment until a day or two before it was due and then pull a few all-nighters, Paula had more discipline than that. She was an A+ student not because she was brilliant, but because she was organized. She'd start on her project tonight.

"You have a choice," intoned Mr. Brown. "If you wish, you can trace back one branch of your own family tree until you get to the person who immigrated to Canada. The bulk of this project will be detailing the historical events that led this ancestor to immigrate."

Mr. Brown's eyes gazed around the class then rested on Bob Maracle at the back. "For some of you, this might be too much to ask. Bob, for example, your ancestors have been here for thousands of years." Bob nodded in agreement. "In your case, you can trace back to a pivotal ancestor and then do research on the key historical events of that era."

"For others of you," Mr. Brown continued, "this would be too easy." He stopped beside Janet, Paula's gymnastics nemesis. "Your parents just moved to Brantford from Ohio two years ago." Chuckles rippled through the class. "You can do the same thing that Bob's doing."

"If you don't want to do a family history, you can choose instead to examine a single ethnic group in Canada and determine the political and cultural reasons for that group's decision to immigrate to Canada.

That didn't sound too hard, thought Paula. Her mother's mother, Gramma Pauline MacDonald, lived in town and Paula saw her every Saturday. But Paula couldn't recall any immigration stories. She had a feeling the MacDonalds had been in Canada for a long long time. Her father's parents had moved to Canada from Ukraine just after World War II. It would be simpler to interview them, she decided. They lived in Toronto, but she would have plenty of opportunity to interview them when her family visited them over the Christmas holidays. In the meantime, she could start picking her father's brain.

"Hey nerd-face, I like your glasses."

Things were not going so smoothly for Paula's younger brother Erik. This was his first day at Ryerson Junior High, and it was also the first day that he'd had to wear his new glasses out in public. Troy Smith towered head and shoulders above and he deftly grabbed the glasses from Erik's face and put them over the bridge of his own nose, bending the gold-wired frames to make them fit.

Erik knew that physically he was no match for Troy. Who was?

"Keep them," said Erik. Then he walked away. Troy was surprised at this reaction. Most kids would've tried to grab them off his face, giving him the chance to taunt them further. This was no fun at all. In disgust, he threw the glasses down and kicked them into the dirt with the toe of his Nike. Erik walked slowly towards the school doors, but let Troy pass him at a faster speed. Once Troy was through the doors and safely out of sight, Erik retrieved his glasses. They weren't broken, but there was a scratch down the middle of the left lens. He cleaned them with the cuff of his sweatshirt, shrugged his bangs out of his face, and put the glasses back on.

He got into his home room just before the late bell rang and sat down at the only desk left. Right beside Troy. "Great," thought Erik. He looked around the classroom as the morning announcements droned in the background. As long as he could remember, Erik had managed to be in the same class with several of his buddies, but when he saw who was in this class, his heart sank. Not a single one he'd consider a friend. This was going to be some year.

The first class was English, and it was held in home room. Next came French. Erik noted with dismay that he again was sitting close to Troy, who gave him a malevolent smirk. When recess came, he searched for his buddies from the other class, but when he found them, it was almost time to go back in. By the time lunch rolled around, Erik was feeling really down.

By fluke, Ryerson was actually closer to his house than Agnes Hodge had been. Even though he had packed a lunch, he decided to go home. He didn't have the heart to walk into the lunchroom friendless and vulnerable.

The house was just around the corner on Oak Street and Erik was home in less than a minute. "Maybe this day isn't totally lost after all!" He spied a familiar mailer from *Computer Gaming World* propped up on the stoop of the front door. Just a week earlier, he had finally saved up enough money for the computer game, *Civilization II,* and had sent away for it. Erik ripped open the package and shouted for joy. It was his anticipated game. Retrieving the house key from under the welcome mat, he let himself in and headed straight up to his room.

His bed was still unmade from the morning and there were items of clothing in various stages of dirtiness scattered about. He brushed off a pair of socks from his computer chair and sat down, loading the CD before he even thought about lunch, getting back to school on time, or anything else.

As the game clicked through the options, Erik opened his lunch bag and pulled out a peanut butter and grape jelly sandwich. He absent-mindedly munched on it as he selected the pre-game customizing options. "Hmmm," he mumbled, "I'll be the Indians and I'll set the age of the earth to five billion years." For climate he chose warm, and for terrain he chose arid. And for other civilizations, he chose the Russians, Japanese, Germans, Americans, Aztecs, and the Carthaginians. He chose the "king" level of difficulty, which was four notches up in a difficulty scale of six. He bit another piece of peanut butter and jelly sandwich and watched as the game adjusted for his choices. The screen went black except for a couple of squares of green terrain in the centre. He moved his men around and gradually the black receded and was replaced by green land, with trees and hillsides. "I hope this isn't an island," he mumbled to himself as he noticed far too many blue squares revealing themselves. "Drat!" he said. It was an island! It was much harder to build a civilization on an island. He knew that much from years of playing the original *Civilization*. He was going to have to develop shipbuilding before he could do anything else. Erik was so mesmerized in game strategy that he didn't hear the front door creak open. He didn't even hear the sound of footsteps coming upstairs.

"Why aren't you at school?"

Erik jumped at the sound of his father's voice. He turned around and regarded the man, who was so tall and muscular that he took up practically the whole doorway. No one who looked at father and son together would ever have realized that they were related. Although his job as a construction supervisor provided him with plenty of opportunity for physical exertion, he supplemented that with a daily six-mile run. Erik noted his father's sweat-covered T-shirt and realized that his father had been able to leave the job site long enough in the middle of the day in order to have an early run. A rare occurrence.

"It's lunch time," replied Erik, waving his sandwich as proof.

"Do you think this is a good way to start off the year?" asked his father, who had grabbed a hand towel from the upstairs bathroom and was mopping off his sweaty brow. He cleared a space for himself on Erik's bed by dumping some more dirty clothes on the floor. "When are you going to clean this mess up?" he asked.

Erik sighed. This was so typical of his father. Nothing he did was ever right. What was so bad about a messy room? And what was so terrible about being home at lunch? You'd think he was an axe murderer, the way his father went on. He couldn't admit the real reason he came home, because his father was decidedly unsympathetic when it came to bullies. Mr. Romaniuk had urged him to take boxing lessons, karate, anything so he could defend himself, but Erik had steadfastly refused. He didn't want to get into that argument again. "I forgot my lunch," he lied. "So I decided to come home and get it."

"Okay," said his father. "But let's not make a habit of this. I want you to make some friends at this new school."

Like that's possible, thought Erik. But he nodded in agreement for his father's benefit.

"When do you have to be back at school?" asked Mr. Romaniuk, glancing at his wristwatch.

"I've got another thirty minutes," replied Erik.

"Well, finish up with that computer stuff then, and come on outside with your old man and we can shoot a few hoops before I jump in the shower." Erik knew better than to argue.

When Emily Romaniuk came home from work just before six o'clock, she was delighted to see that, as usual, her daughter had already begun to make dinner. Potatoes were boiling in a pot on the stove, and the aroma of garlic sausages sizzled from the frying pan. Mrs. Romaniuk removed her red silk jacket and hung it up in the front hall closet and then methodically went through the pile of mail that was neatly stacked beside the telephone in the kitchen.

"You're supposed to call Dr. Del Roy as soon as you can," called Paula as she pulled apart a head of romaine lettuce and arranged the pieces in a glass bowl.

"Oh darn," said her mother. "I meant to call him back before I left the hospital." Emily Romaniuk was the manager of pharmacy at the Brantford General Hospital, and due to cutbacks, pharmacy services for all three local hospitals had been consolidated into hers. Unfortunately, more help didn't come with the added responsibilities. Sometimes it felt like she lived and breathed her job.

Mrs. Romaniuk rooted through the kitchen freezer and drew out a shrimp and Oriental vegetable Lean Cuisine. "Can you zap this for me, honey?" she asked Paula, handing her the package with one hand as she dialed the telephone with the other.

"Why don't you just eat what we have for a change?" asked Paula. "I think you'll like it tonight."

"You know that I don't eat potatoes, hon. And garlic sausages? Seriously! I'll have some of that lovely salad you're making, though."

While her mother finished one phone call and started up with another, Paula got the dishes out and plopped them in the middle of the table. She walked out of the kitchen and over to the foot of the stairs, "Erik," she hollered. "Come down now! Supper will be burnt and you don't even have the table set."

Moments later, Erik loped down the stairs and walked into the kitchen. "Smells good, sis. Are you going to make gravy for the potatoes?"

Paula lifted the lid from the frying sausages and

tilted the pan. There was a fair bit of sausage fat at the bottom of the pan, so she added some water from the kettle and some gravy thickener. "Sure," she said, reaching to tousle her brother's hair, but he darted out of the way in the nick of time.

Mr. Romaniuk had been home for an hour already and just finished mowing the lawn. He sat down at the kitchen table, his powerful chest and arms still sweaty from exertion.

Paula opened a bottle of beer and set it before her father, and then got out a Tab for her mother. She poured Erik a glass of milk and got a tall glass of ice water for herself.

As she placed the food on each plate, Mr. Romaniuk grimaced with irritation. "Emily, why are you eating that crap again?"

"You know I have to watch my weight," replied Mrs. Romaniuk.

"Look at Paula," Erik Romaniuk responded. "She's cut back a bit and now she's almost thin. You could learn a lot from your daughter."

Paula stared down at the food on her own plate and felt her cheeks burn a bright red. She hated it when her parents had this argument, and they seemed to be having it frequently of late. She speared a single round of garlic sausage and carefully chewed, trying to block out the sounds of her parents arguing.

"Good gravy, sis," broke in Erik. Paula looked over at her brother who was enthusiastically digging his fork into a huge mound of gravy-covered mashed potatoes. The sight made Paula feel slightly ill.

She turned to her father, "We got our projects for multicultural history today," she said.

He smiled at her and said, "What's the topic? Not that it matters, I know you're going to ace it as usual."

Paula explained what the possibilities were and how she was interested in interviewing Baba and Dido Romaniuk about their immigration experiences from Ukraine.

Her father shook his head. "I very much doubt you'll get either of them to talk about it," he said.

"Why not?" she asked.

"They had a rough time," her father responded. "Your grandfather especially. He went through some nightmarish events. I don't think you'd be doing him any favours by making him relive them. Just leave it alone, okay?"

Paula agreed, but reluctantly. What was she going to do for her project now?

Emily Romaniuk speared a shrimp with her fork and pointed it at her daughter. "You should interview Gramma Pauline."

Paula shook her head. "Her family must have come over ages ago. Besides, MacDonald isn't exactly a multicultural name."

"That's where you're wrong," said her mother. "Gramma Pauline immigrated to Canada when she was little girl. She's Armenian, you know."

"Armenian?" repeated Paula. "Then my grandfather must have been Scottish." Paula could not recall ever meeting her grandfather. He was probably dead by now, she reasoned. She knew that he had taken off on her grandmother decades ago.

"Your grandfather was Armenian too."

"Then how did he end up with a name like MacDonald?" she asked.

"He was an Armenian orphan, and no one knew his mother or father's name, just his first name, which was Mgerdich, or Johnny in English. He got the name 'MacDonald' because that was the name of his sponsoring family."

How was it that no one had ever told her any of this before? "Do you think Gramma would mind talking to me about how and why she immigrated?"

"I'm not sure how much she even knows," replied her mother. "Why don't you ask her and find out?"

After supper was over, Paula gathered the dirty plates and scraped the excess food into the garbage. This was a job that she always elected to do by herself. There was barely any food left on Erik's plate or her father's. Her mother had eaten every last molecule of her Lean Cuisine. What the rest of the family hadn't noticed was Paula's own plate. She had eaten most of her salad and that single round of sausage. The rest, she scraped into the garbage.

Saturday, September 11

Gramma Pauline lived in a small brick house on Grand River Avenue just two miles away from the Romaniuk residence. On Saturdays, if the weather was good, Paula pulled on her running shoes and jogged over to her grandmother's house in the morning, where they would share a pot of jasmine tea and some good conversation.

She was like nobody else's grandmother. Even in old age she was beautiful, with a certain birdlike fragility. Today, her shock of white hair hung loose — a cloud of ripples down her back, and as always, she wore far too many rings. She had on one of her many brilliantly coloured but mismatched silk palazzo sets — today a crimson tunic and orange pants.

Gramma Pauline was sitting on her wooden verandah swing with her legs curled up under her, sketching with charcoal in an artist's notebook. A pair of gold half-glasses were perched on the tip of her nose, and as her granddaughter jogged into her driveway, her brown eyes sparkled over the rim.

"Hi Gramma," said Paula, slowing her run to a stationary jog as she cooled down. She did her cool down stretches and then walked over to the verandah and gave Pauline a firm hug.

"Honey, it's great to see you," said Pauline, returning the hug. Then she held her namesake at arm's length and looked at her in her revealing shorts and T-shirt. She noticed that Paula was thinner than she had been the week before, but she said nothing.

"Do you want your tea out here, or shall we go inside?" asked Pauline.

"Let's go inside," replied Paula, drying the sweat from her arms with a towel her grandmother had handed her. "I've had enough fresh air for the moment."

Paula loved her grandmother's house. Even though it was at least a hundred years old, it had a huge new picture window in the living room. And what used to be the dining room was now an artist's studio with recently added skylights in the ceiling. Paula breathed in the familiar scent of turpentine as she stepped through the studio door.

When Paula was younger, she used to love sprawling out on the Oriental carpet that adorned the floor of this room and she would watch in fascination as her grandmother stirred paints and deftly applied them to canvas.

Her grandmother had a kitchenette set up in the corner of her studio, and the electric kettle was already on a slow boil. Pauline made the jasmine tea and Paula settled down into the overstuffed sofa on the other side of the room and looked around to see what her grandmother had been up to lately. Her eyes were drawn to a new oil painting. It was an abstract design, and depending on how you looked at it, it was a bouquet of spring flowers, a spiral burst of sunbeams, or just random flecks of colour. Gramma Pauline brought over a china cup of tea and followed Paula's gaze. "That painting is for you, honey. I'll frame it for you once the paint is fully dry."

"Thank you, Gramma, it's beautiful," said Paula. "It's quite a bit different from anything you've painted before."

"That's because I painted it with you in mind."

Paula sipped her jasmine tea and stared into the swirls and bursts of colour in the painting. She didn't quite understand how this painting represented her, but she loved it just the same.

"Gramma, I have a school project about immigration. Would you tell me about how you came to Canada?"

Pauline was silent for a moment, and then she sat down on the sofa next to her granddaughter and stared at her tea. "It's funny you should ask me about it after all this time," she said. "For years I've tried to put the past behind me. But the more I try to forget, the more I seem remember." Pauline set her teacup down, and stared at the carpet at their feet. Paula followed her gaze. Like the new oil painting, the carpet was of a colourful sunburst design. The more you stared at it, the more it changed. Gramma Pauline seemed to be totally absorbed.

"If it's painful for you, we don't have to talk about it ..."

"Actually, it's okay, honey. I'd like to tell you the story, but I seem to only remember flashes of things. I don't know exactly how it happened."

"What do you remember?"

"I can remember arriving at the Georgetown Boys' Farm when I was a girl. My parents had accompanied the first fifty orphaned boys from Armenia. I was the only girl, and I was also the only child with parents. I remember Union Jacks waving when we got off the train. And I remember being given a sandwich. I didn't know what a sandwich was back then, because I had never seen one before in my life."

"Did you like it?"

"It was strange. Canadian bread back then was all white store bought-stuff. It had no taste."

"Do you remember anything about Armenia?"

"Only bits. There was a war. There was no food. And hundreds of children were huddled together in darkness." Gramma Pauline sighed. "That's all I can remember right now."

"Do you know what year you came over?"

"That I remember well. I was seven years old and it was 1923."

The Hunger

Monday, September 13

Paula stopped in to the school library during her spare. If she could find something here about Armenians coming to Canada, she wouldn't have to go downtown.

Her first stop was the computer card catalogue. The system at her school library was not as sophisticated as the one at the public library, but she figured it was worth a try. First, she punched in "Armenia." No hits. She tried "Armenians." Again, no hits. She tried "immigrants" and came up with three books: one on German and Polish Canadians; one called *Strangers at Our Gates*; and one called *Canada: Land of Immigrants.* Noting the dewey decimal numbers, Paula decided to take a look at the books. None of them mentioned Armenians. Not in the chapter list in the front, nor in the index at the back.

She walked over to the reference desk and asked Mrs. MacPherson for some help. "Armenian immigration?" the librarian repeated. "I don't believe we have anything on Armenians." The librarian walked over to her desk and opened a drawer. "Maybe there is something in this, though." She handed Paula a booklet called *The Fiction Fit.*

"What is this?" Paula asked.

"It lists works of fiction on all different subjects," explained Mrs. MacPherson. "Sometimes, it's a good place to start."

Paula took the booklet over to a study carrel and flipped through it. It was a listing put together by the board of education in 1992 of suggested novels for a huge variety of subjects. Scanning down the list, she found a subject heading for "Immigrants." She checked out the reading suggestions, and found *The Apprenticeship of Duddy Kravitz*, *The Joy Luck Club*, *Ragtime*, and other good novels, but there were none about Armenians. This was going to be harder than she thought.

Before heading home, she decided to see if she could find her history teacher and see if he had any suggestions for her. She found Mr. Brown still sitting at his desk in the history room, going over some papers. She tapped gently on the door and walked in when he looked up and nodded at her.

"What's the problem, Paula?" he asked, setting down his pen.

"I'm trying to find information on Armenians immigrating to Canada for my project," she explained, "but I can't find anything in the school library."

"Armenians?" asked Mr. Brown. "Are you part Armenian?"

"Yes," said Paula, "I just found out that my maternal grandmother came to Canada from Armenia when she was a child."

"That should make a very interesting project," said Mr. Brown. "Have you interviewed her about her experiences? That would be the logical place to start."

"I tried," explained Paula, "but she was so young when she came over that she doesn't remember much. Just that there was a war and that she came over with a group of orphans in 1923 and stayed at an orphanage called the Georgetown Boys' Farm."

Mr. Brown shook his head. "Georgetown is just an hour away from here, but I don't remember ever hearing about a Georgetown orphanage. I also don't recall a mass immigration of Armenians."

"Well, I don't think my grandmother would get this completely wrong."

"Neither do I. It's just that I don't know what to suggest. Have you tried looking in the public library?"

"Not yet."

"That might be a place to start. Also, try the Internet."

"Okay," said Paula. "Thanks."

When Paula got home after school, she made a beeline up to her brother's bedroom. She knew that she would find him in front of the computer screen.

"How's it going?" she asked, plopping down on Erik's unmade bed.

"I think I'm going to die," he answered.

Paula looked at the computer screen and tried to make sense out of the game her brother was playing. "What do you mean?"

"I should never have started on the 'king' level," said Erik. "It's impossible for me to win. I started out with 'despotism' as the type of government, but moved into a 'republic' too quickly, and now all the citizens are revolting."

Paula looked at the screen and saw little symbols of people crashing into buildings and destroying things. It seemed silly to get all worked up about a game, but she knew her brother took his games very seriously.

"Do you think you could take a break some time soon and let me look something up on the Internet?"

Paula didn't have a computer. The reason Erik did was because he saved every penny that crossed his palm. Birthday and Christmas money was carefully saved, and odd jobs like snow shoveling and grass cutting added to his stash. He had saved enough a year ago to buy a colour printer and a modem. And then Gramma Pauline sprung for a whole year's worth of Internet access, much to the chagrin of his parents. "Both kids will use it for homework," she declared.

"This game is toast anyway," said Erik, hitting the exit button. "What is it that you want to look up?"

"I want to do a search on MetaCrawler for 'immigration' and 'Armenia.'"

Erik rolled his eyes. "I can't believe that you're starting your project now. It's not due for months! Are you sick?"

"I'm not sick," Paula responded. "I get As because

I start my projects early. I don't leave them to the last minute and get only Bs. Like you."

"I'd rather get Bs and have time for fun things than be a work nut like you," flashed Erik.

"Look," asked Paula with sweet impatience. "Can we just do the search?"

Eric punched in both words and then waited while MetaCrawler searched through six search engines. He got fifty-three hits — most of which were tourism sites.

"That's not right," said Paula. "Try 'Armenia' and 'orphans.'"

This search resulted in 33 hits, primarily youth groups, ads for encyclopedias, and so on, but one site caught Paula's eye. It was a photo collection by a person named John Elder, and the photos were from 1917 to 1919. That would have been during the time that Gramma Pauline was still in Armenia. She would have been a toddler then, Paula calculated. Erik clicked onto the site.

The photos were chilling. There was one of ragged children walking up steps to a feeding station, and another of emaciated children in an orphanage. But the picture that had the most impact on Paula was the last. There was a barren country road, empty — except for the skeleton lying abandoned in the middle of it. Had Gramma Pauline actually lived through all of this horror? It hurt her to imagine her beloved grandmother as a child in these conditions.

What had caused it? And how many loved ones had Gramma Pauline lost? No wonder her memories were sketchy.

Friday, September 17, after school

The nurse gently closed the door behind her. Paula glanced around the examining room, and her eye lighted on the weight scale sitting in the corner. She stepped on the scales. This was the moment of truth! The scales at home could be wildly inaccurate. With expert hands, she quickly adjusted the sliding weights until the scale was balanced. But it couldn't be right! According to this scale, Paula had actually gained two pounds since yesterday. Paula was five-foot-ten and her goal was to weigh one hundred and ten pounds and be just as beautiful as her favourite supermodel, Kate Moss. If this scale was right, then she still had twenty pounds to go. Damn! Tears welled in her eyes and she could feel a sob rise in her throat. She took a deep breath, trying to repress the sob.

She got off the scale and slipped the weights back into the zero position. Paula cringed at the thought of someone finding out how much she weighed. She stuck her head out the examining room door. No one in sight. At least she had a few minutes to compose herself.

As the door closed, she caught her own reflection in the mirror on the back of the door. Paula's hair was a mess, and her cheeks looked fat. She glanced down at the image of her body in street clothes and all she could see were huge thighs. "I can't stand this!" she cried, then pummelled her thighs with her fists. "This is where those extra two pounds have settled."

The door opened and the nurse was back. "Are you all right?" she asked. "I thought I heard someone crying."

"I'm fine," Paula said. "In fact, I feel so much better that maybe I don't need to see a doctor after all."

There was a tap on the door and a young man's voice said, "It's Doctor Tavish. May I come in?"

Dr. Tavish again? Damn! One thing Paula liked about coming to the clinic was that she rarely saw the same doctor twice. They could get so nosy, after all. This would be the second time in as many weeks that she happened to be assigned to Dr. Tavish. She would have to be extra careful with him.

The nurse looked at Paula questioningly. Paula nodded with resignation. "Come on in, Doctor T," the nurse said.

Doctor T wasn't more than five foot two and couldn't have weighed more than a hundred pounds soaking wet. But he had a cute sandy-blond moustache and kind blue eyes. He didn't look like a doctor — he looked like Paula's kid brother playing doctor.

"What seems to be the problem?" Doctor T asked, quickly scanning the top page of her medical history.

"My back hurts."

He motioned for her to get up on the examining table and with firm fingers, he traced the lines of her muscles through the back of her shirt. "Do you remember when the pain started?"

"I was lifting boxes at home," she replied. Paula didn't want to tell him what she had really been doing when her back started hurting — that was none of his business!

"Hmm, if you were lifting boxes, it would have been these muscles that were pulled." He then lightly drew his finger down the middle of Paula's back. She flinched. "You didn't do this lifting boxes." It was a statement, not a question.

"Turn around so that you're facing me, Paula." She reluctantly turned around, dangling her legs over the side of the examining table and looked down at her feet — avoiding his eyes.

"Could you have done this exercising?"

Now there was a good excuse! "That's probably when I did it," she exclaimed. "I do sit-ups every night before I go to bed. What I really need, though, Doctor, is just some kind of pain-killer until it heals up."

Again he did that "Hmmm" thing with the frown.

"Let me see your hands."

She stretched them out in front of her and flinched

slightly when he took one in each of his own. Slowly, he looked at each of her palms as if he were about to read her fortune. Paula had to suppress a giggle. What did this have to do with a sore back?

Then he turned her hands palm down and examined her knuckles.

He looked into Paula's eyes, and without a trace of judgment, asked, "So how long have you been making yourself throw up?

Paula yanked her hands away from him as if she had touched something hot. "What are you talking about?"

"Paula, you exhibit all of the classic signs of an anorexic with bulimic tendencies. Take a look at your hands and you tell me how you got bite marks on your knuckles."

She held them, knuckle up, in front of her and stared. Her traitor hands! The knuckle above each index finger was an angry red, the curved lines of tooth marks clearly visible. "I ... I ... fell."

"You fell on a pair of teeth, did you?" The doctor asked dryly. "There is only one way that you can pull that particular muscle in your back and that's from vomiting. This is a chronic condition associated with bulimia."

Paula was stunned. How could a doctor who looked like he was barely out of medical school be so wise to her tricks? As she sat there clutching her arms close to her body, he flipped through the older pages of her chart.

"Can you get up on the scales for me please?"

Paula did as she was asked, painfully aware of those extra two pounds. Dr. Tavish balanced the sliding weights just as she had done moments before, arriving at the same conclusion. Now he knew how fat she was.

"Paula, since last June, your weight has dropped by twenty pounds!"

"That's because I've been dieting," she replied with impatience.

Doctor T took a step back, and with furrowed blond brows, he eyeballed Paula from the top of her head to the tips of her toes. "You're already bordering on a dangerously low body weight."

Paula almost laughed out loud. His scales had just declared that she'd gained two pounds since yesterday! His stupidity didn't even deserve a reply. She stared angrily at his well-manicured index finger as it tapped thoughtfully on the top page of her chart.

"Paula, this isn't a joke." Doctor T put the chart down on the desk and crossed his arms. Paula stared at the number on the scales. "Would you like me to contact your parents about your problem, or do you think that we might be able to work together to make sure you stay healthy?"

At the mention of her parents, Paula's head jerked up. "You cannot tell my parents about this!"

"Everything all right in here, Doctor T?" The nurse popped her head through the door and looked from Paula to the doctor with a worried expression on her face. "Everything's under control, Nancy," he replied. "I'll be out shortly."

Paula got off the scales and sat down on a chair, her eyes downcast. She felt his finger under her chin. He gently lifted her face until their eyes met. "What will it be?" he asked. "Will we work together?"

What choice did she have? "What do you want me to do?" Paula asked, working hard to control her anger.

"I want to set up a regular weekly appointment with you so we can talk about your problems," he said. "And I want to weigh you once each week to make sure you don't lose any more weight."

Paula watched angrily as Doctor Tavish left the examining room. Now she was supposed to come to this office once a week? And to do what? Talk about her problems? Paula had one problem — and it was that she now had this doctor on her back.

She headed out the door, passing the nurses' desk without making an appointment.

Paula had intended to go to the library from the doctor's office in order to do some research on Armenians, but the confrontation with the doctor had aggravated her so much that she had an urge to eat. She headed home. Unlocking the front door she called out, "Anybody here?" even though she knew that it was only 3:30 and far too early for anyone else to be there. Erik had fliers to deliver right after school every Friday and wouldn't be home for another hour. Her mother was rarely home before six, and even if her father were early, he wouldn't be home much before five.

She opened up the refrigerator and gazed in, but it was filled with her mother's low-fat yogurt and leftovers from last night's dinner. The pantry was equally bereft of snacks.

She reached up to the top shelf and with shaking hands, pulled down a dented coffee canister. She tore the lid off with such fury that she cut her hand, but she was oblivious to the pain. Thank God! There were two twenty-dollar bills left of grocery money. Stuffing the bills into her pocket, she dashed out the front door and headed for the store.

Just a little treat is all I want, rationalized Paula. Maybe a cupcake, or a chocolate bar. She told herself that she took the rest of the money just in case she needed some groceries for the family.

When she got into the store, the first thing she spied was a package of store baked butter tarts, twelve for $4.99. Perfect, she thought. That's all I want. I'll have one butter tart, and the rest will be for the family. Better just look around though, maybe we're out of something at home. She pushed her cart to the dairy aisle and noticed that shelved beside the milk were litre cartons of Caramilk chocolate milk, $1.99

each. A tiny glass of rich chocolate would be good with a butter tart. And Erik could have the rest. She had to walk through the freezer aisle to get to the check-out counter, and on her way there she spied Chocolate Madness Extraordinary ice cream, $5.49 a carton. Who am I kidding? Into the cart it went. Her stomach rumbled as she passed through the bakery section. What the hell, she said to herself, throwing in a chocolate fudge birthday cake with pink and white icing, $8.99; a store baked cherry pie, only $3.79! Oh, garlic bread, only $1.99! Sounds good. Salty. I want something salty. She loped down the snack aisle and grabbed a 240 gram package of ripple potato chips, $3.49 — "great value!" the package exclaimed. Paula agreed. Further down in the snack aisle, she spied Double Stuff Oreo Cookies, $3.49. She threw those into the cart too. Chicken, she mumbled. Nice hot greasy chicken. She ran with her cart over to the deli section and scooped up a steaming rotisserie chicken, just $4.19!

She stopped when she estimated that she had reached her forty dollar limit. When the cashier looked with curiosity at the array of food, Paula said, "It's a birthday party. Mom's got a carload of kids to feed." The cashier handed Paula a few coins in change.

Hugging the two grocery bags to her chest, Paula walked out of the store, careful to appear nonchalant.

At home, her demeanour changed. There was no

longer the need to hide her hunger once the front door closed behind her. Paula dumped the bags onto the kitchen table and ripped them open, letting her precious hoard fall across the table. Her mouth filled with saliva at the sight of so much forbidden food. She opened the tinfoil bag of hot chicken, tore off a piece of meat and shoved it into her mouth. Her greasy fingers slipped as they opened the Caramilk, and then she took a swig. She grabbed a wooden spoon from the cutlery drawer and scooped an enormous spoonful of ice-cream from the container. The chocolate richness of the cold dessert filled her mouth and a shiver of fulfillment coursed through her. Next came the cherry pie. Using the same spoon, she dug right to the centre of it and gorged on a huge serving of cherry filling. She tore open the bag of chips and the Double Stuff Oreos, filling her mouth with cookies and chips together. The salty sweetness satisfied a need deep within her.

It seemed that in a blink of an eye, the food was gone. Paula looked at the devastation with dismay. Chicken bones sat in pools of melted ice-cream. Empty cartons and soiled utensils had scattered over the table and on to the floor.

What have I done? Her hands were sticky with remnants of her feast. She let out a low moan and pounded a fist on the table. Oh God, I am so bad! And to think that the stupid doctor thought I was too thin. This little episode will put ten pounds on me.

She ran to the bathroom, then carefully twisted her long hair into a knot at the nape of her neck so it wouldn't get in the way. She leaned over the toilet and jammed the fingers of her right hand down her throat. The sensation of her teeth grazing her scabbed knuckles brought her up short. What am I doing? She thought desperately. The doctor will know!

She ran back to the kitchen and grabbed the wooden spoon that was still sticky with ice cream, and took it back to the bathroom. Crouching over the toilet again, she shoved the spoon down her throat until she gagged. Her stomach convulsed, and with a lurch forward, huge chunks of undigested food hit the toilet water with such a force that it splashed back in her face. Shoving the spoon even deeper down her throat, she gagged again, this time splashing chunks of undigested food into her hair and down her shirt. Some of the mess landed on the floor around the base of the toilet, and some of it landed all over the space-heater against the wall. The effort sent shivers of exhaustion through Paula's body. She sat on the bathroom floor and hugged her vomit-covered knees tight until her breathing settled down and her heart's staccato beat subsided. She dragged herself to a standing position and looked at herself in the mirror. Her eyes were bloodshot. Mucus hung from her nose. Her throat was raw from the wooden spoon. Her hair and face were wet with toilet water and worse. "You are so disgusting."

Paula tore off her filthy jeans and shirt and climbed into the shower, turning the stream of water on as hot as she could stand it. It was as if she thought she could wash the past hour away. As her guilt swirled down the drain, she dried herself and wrapped her hair into a towel. She pulled on a terry robe and gathered the pile of clothing from the floor and tossed it into the washing machine. To make it less obvious, she prodded around the laundry shute and found a few other items to throw in the wash and make it look like she was just helping out with the laundry. With bathroom cleaner and a rag, she meticulously cleaned the sink, the floor and the toilet. The space heater took more time to clean, because fragments of food had lodged within the grille and between the wall and the heater. By the time she finished, the bathroom was cleaner than before she had purged. Next, she grabbed a garbage bag from the garage and headed back to the kitchen to clean up that mess. She shoveled all the signs of her last meal into the bag and out of sight. She scrubbed the floor and table clean, and placed the bulging bag in between the other garbage bags in the garage. Just as she reached for the handle of the door that led from the garage into the kitchen, Paula was startled to hear the sound of the front door slamming shut. God, is it 4:30 already? She smoothed the front of her robe and took a deep breath, hoping her brother wouldn't notice anything amiss.

"Paula! What happened?" Erik dropped his knapsack in the front hallway and stared at his sister. "Your eyes are all red. Have you been crying?"

Great, thought Paula. So much for not noticing. "I've got a cold," replied Paula, scooting past her brother.

In her top drawer Paula kept a bottle of Visine and a container of matte face powder. The drops stung as they went in, but her eyes quickly lost their redness. Next, she patted powder over the blotchy spots on her face. Paula then changed into a fresh pair of jeans and a T-shirt.

"Never again," she swore to herself. "Never again will I lose control like that!"

Thursday, October 1

It was early morning, and Doctor Tavish sat in the basement office that he shared with two other clinic colleagues. A stack of charts were piled on his desk, a cold cup of coffee on the side. Halfway through the charts, he happened upon Paula Romaniuk's. "Where has she been?" He wrote her phone number on a scrap of paper and stuck it in his shirt pocket. Sipping the cold coffee, he continued working his way through the charts.

At the same time that Doctor T was perusing

Paula's chart, Paula was standing in front of her dresser mirror in her loft bedroom, staring at her reflection with clinical detachment. She slipped off her flannel nightgown and shivered slightly as it fell to the floor. Her eyes darted to the various posters that adorned her walls. Where other girls her age hid the floral wallpaper of childhood with posters of rock stars or school artwork, Paula's choice leaned towards photos of ballerinas, Calvin Klein models, and figure skaters.

There was one framed painting that seemed somehow out of place, propped up on the back of Paula's dresser. It was the oil done by Gramma Pauline. Paula loved that painting. When she looked at it, it was as if she could feel the warmth of her grandmother's love envelop her.

Paula's eyes lifted from the painting and back to her own reflection in the dresser mirror. She turned towards the full-length mirror on the opposite wall to get a better look, then let out a tiny gasp of pride at the tall sleek figure that was her own. She looked back at her posters of models and dancers and smiled. Paula had no reason to feel out of place in this room of well-toned women. Another day had arrived and yet she had still managed to banish more fat and more of the awkward Paula of old.

Reassured by the mirror, Paula stepped on the scale that she kept beside it and watched as the indicator stopped at 126. "Yippee!" she trilled. "Down another pound."

She pulled on a bra and underwear. Zipping up a pair of baggy jeans and pulling a teal-coloured baby T over her head, and her Doc Martens onto her feet, she stood again in front of the mirror and smiled with pride.

Her favourite poster was one of Calista Flockhart, sitting gamine-like on a park bench in a T-shirt and jeans. Paula figured she looked almost as good as Calista.

The heady aroma of bacon reached out and clutched her stomach before she even rounded the corner to the kitchen. In the past year, as her weight dropped from 150 to 126, Paula's sense of smell had become sharper. She walked into the kitchen and saw her mother and father who were already sitting at the table eating breakfast. Erik was no longer there, although his cereal bowl containing a few stray bloated Cocoa Puffs, indicated his recent departure. She knew that Erik was probably sitting on the front steps, playing his Game Gear in solitude — away from the wrath of his father's eyes and waiting until the last possible moment before heading off to school.

Paula's father was savouring his bacon and eggs, while her mother nibbled on a piece of dry toast. Paula poured herself a bowl of toasted oats and sat down at the table with her parents.

Mrs. Romaniuk set down her toast and frowned at her daughter, "Is that all that you're having for breakfast? You'll be starving by mid-morning."

"Leave the girl alone, Em, she's old enough to know what she's doing." Mr. Romaniuk said.

Paula swirled her spoon around the bowl and watched as the little rings of oats bobbed in and out of the milk. She concentrated on the look of her cereal and the smell of her cereal, though she was almost afraid to eat it. By the time her parents had finished their breakfasts and kissed their daughter good-bye, Paula still hadn't eaten. Once both of her parents had left the house, Paula ate one spoonful of what was now mush, then pushed away her bowl.

Paula ran upstairs again and stripped down to her bra and underwear. She stepped back on the scales. Still 126. Thank God, breathed Paula with relief. She threw her clothes back on and left for school.

Paula's daily walk to school always managed to fill her with a quiet sense of joy — even more so since she had embarked on her eating regimen. It seemed that since then, her senses had become sharper. What used to be a simple walk from point A to point B now could be experienced as a feast for the senses. On this fine autumn day, Paula's sense of touch was so acute that she could feel the slightest breeze with her fingertips and could almost count the individual stones of gravel as they crunched below her Doc

Martens. As she passed by her neighbours' houses, her heightened sense of smell identified what each of them had for breakfast. But the best was sight. Grass was electrically green and flowers — even weeds — were outrageously brilliant. Paula savoured the growling of her stomach and gave silent thanks for the choice she had made.

Paula's face was adorned with a radiant smile by the time she walked through the double doors of her high school. She relished the stares of the guys and the covert looks of jealousy from the girls. Thinness was power.

In English class, she listened with rapt attention but was shocked to realize by the end of the period that again, she hadn't absorbed a word. While her eyes were focused on the teacher and what he wrote on the chalkboard, Paula had been distracted by food. She had been imagining that the blackboard was a huge Hershey bar and the chalk was vanilla icing. Her sense of smell was so acute that she could smell breakfast on the lips of the boy beside her — Cream of Wheat sprinkled with brown sugar. It took all of her concentration to stay in her seat and not jump up and lick his lips. She would never do that though, because there was no sense in risking the calories.

She shook her head to try to dispel the colliding images of food. How would she be able to keep up her good marks if she couldn't concentrate? Even when she brought home her usual 90s, her father would ask jokingly, "What happened to the other 10 percent?" She didn't want to even think of his reaction if her marks suffered. Already, she had received a few bad marks, but she had been able to hide that fact from her parents by being very selective in choosing which tests to bring home. She had also become adept at forging her mother's signature. But if she didn't get her act together soon, her parents would find out.

"Hey, Paula! Do you want to go to the mall after school?" At first, Paula didn't even recognize the voice. She could, however, tell that whoever it was had eaten strawberry jam on toast that morning. She looked up and saw her best friend Mandy standing by the side of her desk with a couple of other girls from the class. Mandy's expression was one of mild hurt, although Paula couldn't quite figure out why.

"I can't go tonight, Mans, I've got to exercise." Paula tried to focus on Mandy's angry green eyes, but the scent of strawberry jam was overpowering.

"Suit yourself," said Mandy. "But there are more important things in life than aerobics."

Paula watched as Mandy's cloud of red hair disappeared through the classroom door. Strawberry blonde, she thought to herself, stomach grumbling.

Mandy's just jealous of me, rationalized Paula. She could stand to lose a few pounds herself and she's just mad at me for having more control than she does. Paula waited until the group of girls was down the hallway and then she got up from her desk and walked alone to her next class.

Paula was proud of the fact that she had only purged a few more times since that dreadful appointment with Doctor Tavish. She wanted to lose weight by controlling what she ate, not by vomiting, and she felt that this was a battle she could win. She held her hands knuckles up and regarded them with pride: the scabs had mostly healed. When she did have to vomit, she now used the spoon.

She was so close to her goal that she could taste it.

One thing Mandy wasn't all wrong about, though, was that there was more to life than exercise. Like getting good marks. If she aced that history project, it would make up for the quiz that she daydreamed through the other day. Instead of going to aerobics after school, Paula stopped off at the Brantford Public Library.

She walked up to one of the computer card catalogues on the main floor and chose "keyword subject" and typed in "Armenian history." No hits. She tried "history Armenia." Again no hits. Changing her strategy, she clicked on "general subjects" then typed in Armenia. She got eight hits, all folk lore, music, or travel. Maddening! Using the same "general subjects" search, she typed in "Armenian". As all the usual hits like "music" and "folk lore" popped up on the screen, Paula noticed a new heading:

Armenian Massacres: 1915 – 1923

Massacres? What was going on? From the photos Paula had found on the Internet, she knew that something terrible had happened, but she had assumed it had been a result of the First World War. A massacre was much more sinister. And the years were exactly when Gramma Pauline had been there.

Paula clicked on the "show more" button and a listing for two books appeared: *The Road from Home, The Story of an Armenian Girl* by David Kherdian, and *Passage to Ararat* by Michael Arlen. Paula noted down the call numbers, then headed to the stacks.

She found *The Road from Home* nestled between a traveller's guide to Turkey, and a history of Turkey. This confused her even more. What was an Armenian book doing amongst all these Turkish books? Paula drew the book from the shelf and read two brief paragraphs on the first page:

> *September 16, 1916—*
> To the Government of Aleppo
> It was at first communicated to you that the government, by order of Jemiet, had decided to destroy completely all the Armenians living in

> Turkey ... An end must be put to their existence, however criminal the measures taken may be, and no regard must be paid to either age or sex nor to conscientious scruples.
>
> Minister of the Interior TALAAT PASHA

> *August 22, 1939.* — I have given orders to my Death Units to exterminate without mercy or pity men, women, and children belonging to the Polish-speaking race. It is only in this manner that we can acquire the vital territory which we need. After all, who remembers today the extermination of the Armenians?
>
> ADOLF HITLER

Paula snapped the book shut and held it to her chest. This was all so confusing and upsetting! Extermination of the Armenians? How could she not have heard of this before? Her knees buckled beneath her, and she collapsed in a heap between the aisles, still clutching the book. Her heart pounded wildly and she felt faintly ill. What had her grandmother lived through? As she sat there on the floor, her eyes were drawn back to the gap in the stacks from where she had removed *The Road from Home.* She drew down a book called *Turkey* by Roderic H. Davison and turned to the table of contents, scanning the chapter headings. One was called "From Empire to Republic, 1909–1923" so she turned to that.

She read about the overthrow of the Ottoman Empire's Sultan, Abdulhamid, by the Young Turk revolution, and about the increasing promotion of all things Turkish and the oppression of minorities. She skimmed the pages, trying to find a mention of Armenians. A few pages into the chapter, she found a single paragraph:

> While the battle for Gallipoli was at its height, and while the Russians were pushing into eastern Anatolia, the CUP government began to deport the Armenians.....One of the great tragedies of the war ensued, as more than a half million lost their lives from massacre, exhaustion, malnutrition, and all the hazards of the long march under primitive conditions. Talat, minister of the interior, explained the deportations as a military necessity, since some Armenians were cooperating with the Russians and the danger of revolt behind Turkish lines in the East had to be averted. He admitted that excesses had occurred, and that innocent people had perished.

What shocked her almost as much as the information was the way that the death of so many was brushed off in a paragraph. Paula's whole concept of modern history was crumbling before her. She wrapped her arms around her legs and wept. She wept for her grandmother, and she wept for the thousands whose deaths didn't merit ink on a page. After awhile, she got up off the floor and carefully placed the books back on the shelf. Wiping the tears from her eyes, she walked out of the library.

She was letting herself in the front door when she heard the telephone ringing. Dropping her books in the front hall, she grabbed the phone.

"Is this Paula Romaniuk?" the strangely familiar voice inquired.

"Yes," replied Paula.

"This is Doctor Tavish. I was expecting to see you in my office once a week, remember?"

Doctor Tavish's mildly angry tone mortified Paula. "Oh Doctor T," she said, trying to think of an excuse for her absence. "I've had the flu and couldn't get in to see you." The moment the excuse tumbled from her lips she wished she could have called it back.

The was a pause at the other end of the line and then Doctor Tavish said, "Hmmm, this is the first time I've heard of someone staying away from the doctor's office because they were sick!"

"Really, doctor. Things have been hectic, and I just forgot to come in."

"Remember our deal, Paula. Do you want me to tell your parents about your medical condition?"

Paula's heart pumped with anxiety at the thought of her parents finding out. "Doctor Tavish, I have good news! Since I saw you two weeks ago, I've gained a pound."

"Really?" replied Doctor Tavish in a skeptical tone. "Just the same, I'd like you to come to the clinic tomorrow at four so we can have a little chat."

Erik's day at school had been lousy as usual. His math teacher had paired him up with Troy Smith so that he could tutor him. Unbelievable!

The one positive thing was that when he walked through the door to the house, he could smell something good. Erik couldn't understand how his sister knew so much about food when she was so darned skinny.

Leaving his knapsack in the hallway, he walked into the kitchen to see what she was cooking up this time.

"Kasha," she answered, as Erik lifted the lid to the big pot. "Baba Romaniuk taught me how to make it last year, but I kept on forgetting about it. I just added the broth, so it simmers for an hour and then it's done."

"Does that mean you have time to play some *Civ II* with me?" asked Erik.

Paula hesitated. "Hmmm. How about this? Let

me look up some more stuff on the Internet, and then we'll play for a bit."

"Sure!" Erik grinned. He raced upstairs with his sister close behind.

Erik sat down in his computer chair and then opened up his Netscape Communicator. "What do you want to look up this time?"

"Use MetaCrawler again and search for 'Georgetown Boys' Farm,'" replied Paula, as she cleared a space on his bed and sat down.

Erik punched in the words then chose the option, "exact phrase," then hit "go." It timed out with no hits.

"Try 'Armenian Massacre.'"

"*What*?" asked Erik.

"I was just at the library today trying to look up stuff about Armenians and I ran across all these references to a massacre. Apparently, more than half a million Armenians were rounded up in Turkey and killed."

"Are you sure?" asked Erik. "Don't you think we would have heard about this in school if it really happened?"

"You'd think so," said Paula.

Erik keyed in the phrase and hit "go."

Seconds later, MetaCrawler showed twenty-five hits. Scrolling through the choices, Paula found constant references to 1.5 million dead, not half a million. This was all so confusing! She pointed to a site called "The Armenian Genocide: Dr. Martin Piege's Report." Erik clicked onto it.

As Erik clicked through the options on the site, he happened upon one called "pictures." He clicked on that and grainy photographs began to form. The caption on the top explained that these were photos taken by a German officer in Aleppo in 1915. As one photo came into focus, Paula shuddered. An emaciated young woman with long dark hair piled on the top of her head lay dead, her arms embracing the corpses of two skeletal children.

Gramma Pauline was born in 1916 — right in the midst of the worst assaults on the Armenians in Turkey. How could an Armenian baby have been born at that time? Paula couldn't imagine the conditions that must have confronted her own great-grandparents.

Erik exited from the site back to the list of hits. This time, Paula chose one called "Armenian genocide: personal narratives." Erik clicked on that site, and a page worth of names popped up, each one leading to a personal story. Paula chose one close to the bottom of the page and read how the writer's great-grandmother had been sold to a Turkish family and worked as a slave. One phrase at the bottom of the narrative stood out. The woman said, "When Hitler was planning his genocide in the 1930s, his rationale was, 'Who today remembers the Armenians?'"

That same quote. Paula was stunned by it because

the woman was right even now. Who today remembers what happened to the Armenians? Not her history teacher, and not the school librarian either. Even Gramma Pauline, who had been through it, said she had only sketchy memories.

"Do you think Gramma was one of the Armenians going through all of that?" asked Erik as he scrolled through story after story.

"She was," replied Paula. "And she was just a child too. Can you imagine how horrible her life must have been?"

"No," said Erik. "Sure puts our problems in perspective."

"You're right," said Paula. "It's not like we have life and death situations to deal with."

Erik closed Netscape and disconnected the modem, then popped in the *Civ II* CD.

"Are you starting a new game?" asked Paula, still trying to shake the frightening images from her mind.

"Yep. I can customize it. Any suggestions?"

"Sure," said Paula. "Can you make us the Armenians?"

"When you customize the game, you can be anyone you want." Erik scrolled through the options one by one. "Okay," he said. "We're the Armenians, and you're Paula, leader of the Armenians." Erik scrolled through other choices, "What do you want the temperature to be? Cool, temperate, or warm?"

"Let's make it warm."

"Okay. How about the climate? It can be arid, normal, or wet."

"Let's choose arid."

"Okay. What other civilizations do you want?"

"Can we choose Turks?"

"Nope. That's not one of the choices. Even if you customize the game, you can only choose from the game's list of civilizations for everyone but your own."

"Hmmm," said Paula. "Then why don't we make the other civilizations the English, Germans, and Russians."

"Okay." Erik could hardly contain his excitement. It was like the old days with Paula sitting here, playing a computer game with him.

"What level are we going to play it on?" asked Paula.

"We're sure not going to play it on 'king' again," he said. "Level one is 'chieftain.' It's way too easy. Maybe we should play it on 'prince,' which is one level down from 'king.'"

"Sounds good," said Paula. Then she watched the screen as the game computed all the choices that they had made.

The screen went black except for a couple of green squares in the middle. As Erik made moves with his mouse, more squares opened up. "Good!" shouted

Erik. "At least we're not an island this time."

"Are you looking for a good place to put your capital city?" Paula asked, remembering how it worked in the original *Civilization.*

"Yes. I want to put it somewhere on land, not close to an ocean because you can get attacked too easily if it's close to an ocean."

"What about here?" Paula pointed to a flat area of land close to a river.

"That's pretty good," said Erik. "It's got the river, making it easier for irrigation and transportation of resources. That's actually a very good site. Thanks, sis."

Paula sat and watched as her brother flashed through turns. He played the game so rapidly that she had trouble keeping track of everything he did. As the land masses revealed themselves, populations increased and years went by. The form of government changed from despotism to monarchy, and technology evolved through ritual burial, writing, literacy, iron working, invention of the wheel, horseback riding. Paula's eyes glazed over as she watched the choices flicker by. They played until Paula detected the sharp smell of burning kasha. She ran downstairs to see if she could salvage supper.

Friday, October 2, after school

Paula didn't go directly from school to the clinic. She stopped at home and drank six huge glasses of water, only stopping when she thought she might throw up. She checked her weight on the scale in her room and was gratified to see that it showed her at 128. Rooting around in her sock drawer, she pulled out a set of flexible wrist weights. She slipped these on and found a long-sleeved sweater in her closet and pulled it over her head, rolling the cuffs to hide the weights.

"One hundred and thirty one pounds," declared Dr. Tavish.

Paula smiled to herself. For once, the scales had become her ally.

"I still want you to come in next week, Paula," said Doctor T, writing out instructions on a prescription sheet. "And this time, I'll come out with you to the nurses' desk and help you schedule that appointment."

Paula rolled her eyes in disgust, but followed behind him.

Friday, October 9 — 122 pounds

Paula always felt cold. Throughout most of September, the weather had been moderately cool, and Paula's layering of clothing for warmth and subterfuge had gone unnoticed. But Indian summer had arrived with a vengeance, and today was unseasonably hot. Paula dug through her drawer and found a wraparound denim mini skirt that had been one of her favourite pieces of clothing just a year before. She held it up to her waist and walked to the mirror, chuckling at how huge the skirt looked now. She could still wear it, but it would require a lot more "wrapping around" than it did last year! Before she put it on, she stepped onto her scales and was delighted to see that the weight was still coming off. She hoped that the weather would cool down by her four o'clock appointment with Doctor Tavish; otherwise, he'd be suspicious of her bulky clothing.

When Paula walked into the kitchen that morning for breakfast, her brother Erik was sitting by himself at the table, immersed in his portable video game. His bowl of Cocoa Puffs was pushed to one side, the cereal bloated with neglect. Her father had already left for work and her mother was still in the shower. At the sight of his sister in her revealing outfit, Erik dropped his Game Gear on the table with a clatter.

"When did you get so skinny, Paula?" he asked.

Paula flashed him a hurt look and then walked over to the counter and poured herself a cup of black coffee.

"I'm serious, Paula. You look like that mother we found on the Internet last night."

"That's a nasty thing to say to your sister," Paula

replied, then took her mug back over to the table and sat down. For several minutes she simply sat there, breathing in the aroma of fresh coffee. Sometimes, she thought, smelling was as good as eating.

When she slipped home just before her four o'clock doctor's appointment, Paula realized she had a problem. Temperatures had remained high all day and there was no way she would look normal wearing bulky clothes. Where could she hide her weights? Her sessions had been going on for a number of weeks, and as the time passed, Paula had become adept at hiding weights in various places within her clothing. Doctor Tavish had congratulated her on maintaining her weight of 131 pounds. This feat of deception became harder as her real weight declined.

Paula forced herself to drink more water than she ever had before — nine glasses! And she felt like she could barely walk without slishing and sloshing. She fanned out her array of weights on the bedspread and tried to decide which ones would be most hideable under light clothing. In the end, she wore a five-pound belt tied around her waist and underneath an untucked blouse.

She stepped on the scales. One hundred and twenty nine. Good.

Paula rarely had to wait more than fifteen minutes for her session with Doctor Tavish, but today he seemed to be taking forever. By the time the clock showed 4:30, Paula was in agony. She had to go to the bathroom or she would burst. Clutching her stomach, Paula walked up to the nurses' desk and asked Nancy how much longer the doctor would be.

"Oh Hon," said Nancy, looking up a stack of forms. "He got called out to deliver a baby and he's been behind schedule ever since."

"Maybe I should skip this appointment and come back next week," said Paula, trying her best not to hop from one foot to the other.

"No," said Nancy. "Doctor T gave me specific instructions. He told me to ask you to wait. He'll be no more than another fifteen minutes."

Nancy watched as Paula ran to the bathroom.

Knowing she couldn't hold it any longer, Paula peed what felt like gallons of water. As she sat on the toilet, she considered her options. If she took off without waiting to see Doctor T, he'd call her parents. If he saw her and weighed her as usual, he'd discover her deception.

Paula's only solution was to drink more water before she was called in for her appointment.

When Paula left the bathroom, she made a beeline for the cooler in the corner and rapidly downed half a dozen tiny cones of water — equaling about one glass of water at home.

As she waited for the seventh to fill up, she heard

Nancy call her name. "Damn!" she muttered. There's no way I'll weigh enough. She quickly gulped a last cone of water, then followed Nancy into one of the examining rooms.

"You must be thirsty today," said Nancy. Paula could only hope that she wouldn't mention anything to Doctor Tavish.

As Paula sat on the edge of the examining table waiting for the doctor to arrive, she breathed a nervous sigh. She knew that this was the day she would be found out. After a few minutes of waiting, she heard low voices just outside her door. Nancy tattling on her, Paula thought with anger.

Doctor Tavish tapped on the door, then opened it a crack. "Paula, I'd like you to change into a hospital gown for your weighing today," he said. "Let me know when you're ready for me to enter."

A hospital gown? Paula lifted one of the worn blue gowns from a pile on the table and held it in front of her. This was worse than she had imagined. Paula couldn't possibly hide her waist weight in an open-backed hospital gown.

She was trapped.

Paula threw the blue gown onto the floor of the examining room and opened the door. "Screw this," she thought. "No matter what I do, they're going to tell my parents."

She walked down the hallway, passing Nancy and

Doctor Tavish, who were huddled in deep conversation. Doctor Tavish looked up as Paula walked past him. "Hold on!" he said. "We can help you."

"I don't need help," said Paula, as she walked out the doors of the clinic.

Paula was thrown into another state of hungered frenzy. She ran home from the clinic and opened the pantry door. She pulled down the coffee canister and pried off the lid. "Damn, damn, damn!" There was no money.

Paula loped up the stairs to her brother's room at the end of the hallway. She opened his door and was relieved to see that he wasn't there. "He must be late with his fliers," she considered. It was almost five o'clock. Later than usual for her brother to be gone. She lifted up the bottom corner of her brother's duvet and groped under the mattress, looking for his stash of bills.

"Ouch!" she yelped, withdrawing her hand. A mouse trap dangled from her index finger. "You jerk," cried Paula. Leave it to her brother to protect his money with a lethal weapon.

Paula pried her finger loose and threw the trap on the floor into a pile of her brother's clothing. "I hope you step on it, you little twerp," she muttered under her breath.

She dashed down the stairs and ran into the kitchen, opening the pantry door wide, looking for something, anything to gorge on. But her mother's diet regimens had stripped the selection down to only the barest of choices.

Paula grabbed a bag of brown sugar, the canister of flour, a package of lard, and some chocolate syrup. Getting out a bowl and her trusty wooden spoon, she dug out a dollop of the lard and dumped it into the bowl. She mixed alternating spoonfuls of flour and sugar, stirring all the while to maintain an icing-like consistency. When the full container of lard had been worked into the mixture and most of the sugar was gone, Paula squirted a stream of chocolate syrup over it. Paula dipped her spoon into the sludge and filled her mouth.

At precisely that moment, Paula's mother entered the kitchen.

"What are you doing?" Her mother walked over to where she was sitting and grabbed the wooden spoon away from her mouth. She dropped the spoon on the table, splattering Paula with the chocolatey mess. Paula didn't know whether she was more stunned by the confrontation or by the simple fact that her mother was actually home before 6.

"I ... I'm ... hungry," she said quietly.

"If you're hungry, I can make you something healthy." Mrs. Romaniuk's voice had a shrill undertone of panic. She walked over to the pantry and opened it much like her daughter had done moments before.

Scanning the shelves for something to offer, she said, "I can warm up some soup. Or how about crackers? There's cheese in the fridge. I know we've got apples."

"Forget it, Mom. I'm fine," Paula said, pushing the bowl of calories away from her.

Emily Romaniuk walked back over to the table and sat in the chair across from her daughter. "You're not fine," she said. "I got a call from Dr. Tavish today." Tears welled in her eyes as she continued. "When he told me he was calling about you, I was so afraid that something serious had happened to you, and then when he told me it was about your diet, I was confused. He says you're anorexic with bulimic tendencies. Is that true?"

"No, it's not true," said Paula. "He thinks I should weigh more, that's all."

"That's not all, honey," responded Mrs. Romaniuk. "Dr. Tavish told me that we should all go into therapy." With that, her voice cracked, and Mrs. Romaniuk held her face in her hands. "How could I let this happen?"

"Mom," responded Paula in alarm. "You didn't do anything! It's all Dr. Tavish's fault. He has unrealistic expectations about what I should weigh. Did you know that I haven't lost a single pound since I've been seeing him?"

As soon as the statement was out, Paula wished she hadn't said it. Her mother looked at her face and then at her arms. She looked under the table at

Paula's bony legs. "He says you've been tricking him with water-loading and wearing weights." It was a statement, not a question, so Paula didn't reply.

"I want you to weigh yourself right now, Paula. And I will watch."

Slowly, the two walked up the flight of stairs to Paula's bedroom. Her mother stood in the doorway as Paula gingerly stepped on the scales.

The indicator wavered back and forth, finally settling on 121. Paula almost leapt for joy at the loss of another pound, but remembered that her mother was standing there and that she wouldn't be impressed.

"Doctor Tavish says you should be hospitalized if you get below 115," her mother said with a tremor in her voice. She was deeply shocked by the number on the scale. She knew that the normal range for a teenager of Paula's height should be 140 to 165 pounds. "We'll have to start family counselling immediately if we want to avoid hospitalization."

Paula looked up from the scales, "Don't you think we can work on this together?" she asked. "We should at least give it a try before we give up and go into therapy." Her mother's brows furrowed as she considered this new option. Paula smiled inwardly. She always had been good at pushing the right buttons.

Paula stared down at a dinner plate of steak, potato salad, and creamed corn that her mother had made and placed before her. She could feel the bile in her throat rise at the sight of such fattening fare.

"You have to eat every bite," said her father, who was eating his dinner with gusto. Her brother Erik also seemed thrilled with the menu.

Paula looked over at her mother, who was picking at her plate. Her mother looked up and met the pained expression in her daughter's eyes. She carefully placed her fork beside her plate and said to her husband, "Erik, I don't think Dr. Tavish meant for us to force Paula to eat."

"Emily," said Mr. Romaniuk, "He told us if she didn't start gaining back some weight, she'd have to be hospitalized."

"I know that. I talked to him, too. What he suggested is that we all go to counselling together so that we can get to the bottom of this problem. Force-feeding isn't the solution."

"Look," said Mr. Romaniuk, "I am not going to sit in a room listening to some ninety-dollar-an-hour social worker who drinks coffee all day for a living. If our daughter needs to put some meat on her bones, we can do that ourselves. Without interference." Paula's father speared a piece of steak and popped it into his mouth, chewing thoughtfully. "You could help, Emily, if you were a better role model for your daughter."

"What is that supposed to mean?" answered Mrs. Romaniuk.

"Stop eating all that diet food. What do you think gave her the idea in the first place?"

"That's easy for you to say," her mother flashed angrily. "You know that I've had trouble keeping my weight down ever since I had the kids."

During this conversation, Paula hung her head guiltily. It was giving birth to her that had made her mother fat in the first place. And now it was because of her that her parents were having this big blow-up.

She dug her fork into the heap of potato salad and pulled out a chunk. She swallowed back the bile that had accumulated at the back of her throat and placed the food onto her tongue. The weight of it made her want to gag — the oily texture of mayonnaise-laden potato chunks was making her feel more nauseated by the moment. She made chewing motions with her mouth. She desperately wanted to make her parents happy, but she felt incapable of eating this food. She wished that her parents would be distracted so she could spit the obscene mess out of her mouth and into her serviette.

"You'd better swallow that, sis, before it starts sprouting," Erik teased.

Paula's father made her finish every last bite of food on her plate. When she asked to be excused, he wouldn't let her get up. "You're just going to vomit," he explained. "That's what bulimics do." He took off his wristwatch and set it in front of him on the table, then opened the sports section of the newspaper. “You can get up in half an hour.”

Paula felt trapped and humiliated. The food that he had made her eat was sitting in the pit of her stomach, just waiting to be thrown up. She could feel a bulge forming on her once-flat stomach as she imagined the unnecessary calories being absorbed into her system. She had to get away!

“I have a history test tomorrow, Dad, and I've got to study.”

“Erik!” her father hollered. “Bring down your sister's knapsack.” He turned to look at her. “No reason you can't study while you wait.”

When the half hour was up, Paula knew better than to run to the bathroom to try and throw up — her father would hear everything. Instead, she went to her room, closed the door, and rooted through her top drawer. Stashed in the back was her emergency supply of laxatives. She swallowed a triple dose.

She then began a frenzied series of sit ups. One calorie per sit up, she figured, and that meal must have had at least 1200 calories.

Monday, October 26, 114 pounds

Paula gave her room one last glance, then picked up her overnight bag and walked down the stairs. Doctor

Tavish had warned her that the hospital did not allow much in the way of personal items. No make-up or stuffed animals. She had packed a couple of novels, sweat pants and shirts, underwear, and shampoo. The bag was not heavy, but to Paula it felt like it held the weight of the world.

Her parents and brother were already waiting in the car, so Paula didn't linger as she walked through the front room and out the door to the driveway.

Because she was still only 15, Doctor Tavish had her admitted onto the pediatric ward. Homewood, a hospital just one hundred kilometres away in Guelph, had a very successful eating disorder treatment program, but it also had a waiting list more than a month long. Doctor Tavish wouldn't risk waiting any longer. He put her on the waiting list for Homewood, but admitted her to Brantford General immediately.

As Paula walked through the hospital corridor with her parents on either side and her brother trailing behind, she couldn't help but notice some of the other children on the ward. Two preschoolers who looked like they had been beaten were now wrapped in gauze and casts in a room to her left. Images of Armenian orphans flashed through her mind. Across the hallway was a boy in traction with a broken leg. Three children ran up and down the hallway, shrieking excitedly. One bumped into Paula and almost knocked her over. "Lady, you're dead skinny!" the young boy said, looking at Paula in disgust. Her father gripped her arm protectively and shook his finger at the boy. "Mind your own business," he blurted.

They walked up to the nurses' station opposite the sun room and Mr. Romaniuk said to a nurse who was writing a note in one of her charts, "Excuse me, could you tell me which room my daughter should go to?"

The nurse looked up from her work and regarded the family in front of her. When her gaze lighted on Paula, she said, "You're Doctor Tavish's patient, Paula Romaniuk, right?"

She nodded.

"And I'm Jean Bowley," replied the nurse. We've saved you a private room." And with that, she stood up and motioned them to follow her down the hallway. As Paula followed, she felt like she was walking to her death, but she obediently did as she was told.

The room was stark and white. The only homey touch was a row of plants that looked like they hadn't been watered in decades. The room did, however, have a large picture window. Brilliant midday light streamed through. Paula walked to the window and looked out. A perfect view of the parking lot and not much else.

Nurse Bowley turned to Paula's parents, then stated, "I'm going to have to ask you to leave. Our new patient needs solitude."

Mrs. Romaniuk looked up with alarm. "But can't at least one of us stay here to keep her company?"

"No," replied the nurse. "Paula will have to gain some weight before she earns visitor privileges."

She gave a small wave as the nurse shooed her parents down the hallway.

Erik lagged behind, standing at the side of her bed with one eye to the door, waiting for the nurse to come back and shoo him away. "I brought you something," he said, retrieving a bag from beneath his shirt. "Hide this under your pillow," he shoved the package into her hands. With that, Erik dashed to the door just as the nurse was opening it in search of him. He turned and winked at his sister as his head disappeared through the doorway. "Get better, Paula," he called in parting, "I want my old sister back."

Paula just had enough time to stash the package underneath her pillow before the nurse was back in her room. "Now Paula," she began. "I'll explain the rules here. You get weighed first thing every morning — before breakfast, but after you've been to the bathroom. You'll be weighed in a hospital gown so you can't fool us. And until you've gained ..." Nurse Bowley drew out a chart from the holder on the door, opened it, and frowned. "Okay, it says here that you've got to remain in bed until you've gained two pounds." She looked up from the chart and regarded her new patient.

"I can't do that," stated Paula. "I need my exercise."

The nurse chuckled. "Don't even think about exercising right now." Then she took Paula's overnight bag from her hands and said, "You can have this back once you've gained those two pounds."

Paula looked alarmed. "But what am I supposed to wear? And what am I supposed to do?"

"You'll find a fresh hospital gown in the closet. And all you're supposed to do right now is conserve your energy, sleep, and eat." Then the nurse frowned and shook her head slightly. "I don't think you realize how serious your condition is."

With that, the nurse headed towards the door. When she was almost out, she turned and said, "Slip into that gown now. I'll be back in a few minutes to hook up your IV."

"IV?"

The nurse looked surprised at Paula's reaction. "Of course. We've got to get some nourishment into you quickly. This is no joking matter."

Paula watched as the large pink rear end of Nurse Bowley disappeared through the doorway. "That's what I'll end up looking like," she whispered to herself. "There's no way they're going to make me fat." And then she silently pounded her fists on the bed. "Has the whole world gone crazy?"

A few minutes later, Paula watched as Nurse Bowley tried to insert an IV needle into her forearm for the third time. "Your veins have all but collapsed," said the nurse as she gently tapped Paula's skin to try and find a good vein. "Success!" She noted with approval a drop of blood formed in a bead at the top of the plastic tubing that was attached to the needle. Deftly, the nurse slipped the narrow plastic sleeve over the needle and compressed the end between her finger and thumb, sliding the tubing into the opening made by the needle and slipping the needle out through the other end of the tubing. Securing the tubing in place with a strip of surgical tape, she attached the open end to an IV drip.

Paula could hear the cheerful voice of Nurse Bowley going over the rules of the ward and mentioning something about a menu, but she wasn't really listening. Instead, Paula held her arms up to her face and stared at them. The knuckle scabs had all but healed, leaving a trail of angry red scar tissue in their wake. She lightly drew her right index finger over the bruised spots on her arm where Nurse Bowley had tried to find a vein. This ordeal of being admitted to the hospital was like a war, she realized. And only she knew what — or who — was the real enemy.

When Paula was certain that Nurse Bowley was finished tormenting her for the moment, she reached underneath her pillow and drew out the package her brother had given her. Inside the bag was Erik's beloved Game Gear and it was loaded with the game *Columns* — one that she knew he hated, but one she had always loved for its calming effect. Her eyes welled up with tears. She knew what a sacrifice it was for him to lend her this unit. Without it, he would not be able to play games during the stolen moments of solitude throughout the day. She had ignored him so much during the past year, and when she did pay attention to him, it was to snark at him, yet he was so forgiving. She vowed to be a better sister when she got out of this place. She turned the volume down low, and played a few games in tribute to her brother.

Long after Nurse Bowley's shift had ended, Paula lay curled in the middle of her bed, knees drawn up to her chest, her long skinny arms wrapped around them. She felt orphaned and alone.

She had not bothered to turn on the lights when it began to get dark. It was the wee hours before dawn, and yet she still lay, curled into almost nothing, in the dark. Headlights from an occasional car would momentarily illuminate the room, and when this happened, Paula would stare at the drip dripping of the IV. She felt so powerless, so out of control. It was humiliating to have others determine what shape her body would take. As the drips of clear fluid coursed down the tubing and into her veins, Paula began to form a mental picture of the effects it would have on her body. She imagined her rear end growing to the size of Nurse Bowley's and shuddered. It would be better to die than to live looking like that.

She ran her index finger along the bump in her forearm where the dreaded nourishment was entering. "I should just pull this out," she whispered to herself, tugging gently at the adhesive tape holding the tubing in place. She felt the length of the tubing until her fingers lighted upon a plastic contraption half way up. She held it up to her eyes and waited for a car to pass so she could see what it was. "A clamp!" She turned the clamp shut tight and then noticed with satisfaction that the fluid was no longer finding its way into her veins.

Then she lay down on her pillow and fell asleep.

She was startled awake a few moments later by a knock on her door. The night nurse burst through and turned on the light. Paula rubbed her eyes in the glare of brightness. "What's going on?" she asked.

"Something's happened to your IV," the nurse said, striding over to the bedside and held up the tubing attached to Paula's arm, examining it carefully. Close to where it entered Paula's arm was a faint stain of blood. She traced it from that point to the clamp that had been shut off. She flicked it back on, then rested her eyes on Paula. "This isn't a good way to start out, Paula."

Paula's face flushed with embarrassment.

"Your IV is monitored at the nurses' station. Please don't try to trick us again." With that, the nurse was gone.

Paula lay back down on her bed and tried to fall asleep, but the feeling of powerlessness made her want to scream. She sat back up and drew out her brother's game unit from under her pillow. Sorting through the coloured balls and arranging them in a pattern as they floated down the video screen gave her comfort. Soon she felt settled enough to fall asleep.

She dreamed she was an orphan, marching in the desert. Her feet were covered with rags, and her shirt and pants were tattered and dirty. She looked up and saw hundreds ... no ... thousands ... of people in the same circumstances. Old people left on the side of the road to die; soldiers with bayonets riding horses and terrorizing the column of deportees. She looked into the face of one of the soldiers. There was hatred in his eyes.

Early the next morning, she was startled awake by a knock on her door. "Time to get up!" trilled an unfamiliar voice. "I'll be back to weigh you in five minutes."

Paula sat up and rubbed the sleep from her eyes. A slim twenty-something woman whose blonde hair was swept up into a French twist walked into the room. "Hi Paula," she said. And without further words, she led Paula to the end of the hallway, her IV drip still attached, to weigh her. She wrote down without comment the fact that the patient had gained no weight during her first night in hospital.

Paula walked back into her room, pushing the IV holder before her. When she opened her door, she was surprised to see Gramma Pauline perched on the end of her bed, wearing a volunteer smock. Beside her sat a tray of food.

"What are you doing here, Gramma?" asked Paula, filled with confusion and delight. "I thought visitors weren't allowed."

"Do I look like a visitor?" Pauline asked, pointing to her polyester mauve smock with her name embroidered on the pocket. Her white hair was braided loosely down her back and her hands were surprisingly jewel-free. "I hold a painting workshop for the children up here once a week. This happens to be my regular day."

Paula nodded in understanding. Her grandmother had several pet projects around town, all somehow involving her passion for painting. Paula pointed at the tray of food sitting on the bedside table. "Did you bring that with you?"

Gramma glanced over at the tray of food. "No. I followed it in," she said with a grin. "Now come over here and give me a hug."

Paula gingerly wrapped her arms around her grandmother, taking care not to tangle her IV in the embrace. She breathed in deeply the comforting "Gramma" scent of turpentine and Dove soap, then settled in on the bed beside her grandmother. "I am so glad to see you," Paula said, tears welling up in her eyes.

"I could have picked a better place for the visit, my dear," said Pauline, with sadness tingeing her voice. "I wish you could understand how much you're loved."

With that, Pauline stood up from the bed and brushed her hand gently across her granddaughter's cheek. "Now you owe me a visit."

Paula watched as the mauve smock exited the door.

Her eyes drifted over to the tray of food sitting at her bedside. On it was a glass of orange juice, a carton of whole milk, a muffin, a container of yogurt, and a bowl of bran cereal. The sight of so much food overwhelmed her with a sense of powerlessness. They couldn't possibly expect her to eat all of this. She sat, staring at the tray for several moments, then the door opened again. It was a nurse.

"The more you eat, the quicker you get out of here," said the nurse. "You don't have to eat it all, but do the best you can." Without waiting for a reply, the nurse opened the door. She turned to Paula and said, "Remember. No funny stuff."

Paula poured the milk onto her bran cereal and methodically stirred it until it became mush. She took a single spoonful of it and put it in her mouth, feeling nauseated as she did it. They couldn't force her to eat, that was for sure. It would make her sick.

As trays came back, day after day, barely touched,

the nurses became worried. Doctor Tavish was worried too. But there was nothing they could do. And while treatment for anorexia included the denial of privileges until weight was gained, Doctor Tavish was vehement in his views on force-feeding. "It's counterproductive," he told the nurses. "The more you push an anorexic, the more stubborn they become."

Monday, November 9, 111 pounds

Paula's condition alarmed both Doctor Tavish and the nurses.

The nurses had become so concerned with Paula's condition that they had taken to offering her chilled tins of Ensure, and were gratified when they noticed the empty cans in Paula's garbage. What the nurses didn't notice was how healthy Paula's plants had become.

A social worker who counselled a local eating disorder support group was called in to see if she could help.

She tapped on Paula's door just after lunch had been served. Paula had enough time to stash her brother's Game Gear under her pillow and call out, "Come in, please."

Paula appraised the woman as she stepped through the door. Betty Doherty didn't look like someone who dealt with eating disorders. The fact was, she was definitely on the hefty side herself. "Can I sit down here?" she asked, pulling up a chair beside Paula's bed without waiting for a reply. She settled a briefcase on her lap, then opened it, pulling out a questionnaire. "Mind if I ask you some questions, Paula?"

Paula had the feeling that her answer didn't matter much, but she nodded anyway.

"Okay, let's get down to business," said Mrs. Doherty. "How would you describe the relationship you have with your mother?"

"We have a good relationship."

"And how about with your father?"

"Good too."

"Is there anything you'd like to tell me about your relationship with your father?"

"What do you mean?"

"I don't mean anything. I'm asking a simple question."

Paula rolled her eyes with impatience. "If you're wondering if my father has ever touched me sexually, the answer is no. If you're wondering whether my parents beat me, the answer is no."

"I didn't ask that Paula. And there's no need to be defensive," the social worker answered. "I'm just trying to help you."

"Look," replied Paula. "You're on the wrong track. Why are you even asking me these questions?"

Mrs. Doherty was silent for a moment, considering her answer. "Do you want me to be frank, dear?"

"Yes."

"The vast majority of anorexic teens that I see come from dysfunctional families. Many have been physically or sexually abused. I'm trying to find out whether your family falls into the typical mould."

Paula could feel anger boiling up inside of her. While sometimes she felt that her parents had very high expectations of her, and that sometimes they were a bit too controlling, that was it. Sexual abuse? Beating? This was outrageous.

"Is this what your clients tell you?" asked Paula.

"Not always," replied the woman.

November 23, 111 pounds

While still precariously low, Paula's weight had remained the same for two full weeks. Paula put up with the almost daily sessions with Mrs. Doherty, in the belief that she might get out more quickly if she seemed co-operative.

Today when Mrs. Doherty arrived, she brought a roll of paper, scotch tape, scissors, and a magic marker.

"What's that for?" asked Paula.

"We're going to do a visualization technique," explained the social worker. "I will tape a sheet of this up to the wall and you will lean up against it and I will trace your silhouette."

Paula looked at the roll of paper and saw that it was just two feet wide. "There is no way that you'll be able to trace me on a single roll," she said. "You'll have to tape two sheets together to fit all of me in."

Mrs. Doherty nodded in understanding. "We could fit two of you on this one sheet, Paula. One reason that we do this is because anorexics are not able to see how thin they have become. By tracing you on this paper, I will be able to show you with something concrete just how thin you are."

Paula was skeptical, but she got out of bed and helped the social worker tape a length of paper to the wall and then she stood against it. Mrs. Doherty traced her shape and then Paula stood back to look.

"There's no way that's me!" cried Paula, looking at the emaciated form traced on the paper. "You made it smaller on purpose."

"You don't have to take my word for it," replied Mrs. Doherty, handing Paula the scissors. "Cut the form out."

Paula did as she was told.

"Follow me," said Mrs. Doherty. She had carefully rolled up the paper Paula form, and was carrying it in her hands. Together, they walked down the hospital corridor and into the children's playroom. It was empty. In the corner was a full sized mirror. The social worker unrolled the image of Paula and taped it to the mirror.

"Step in front of the mirror, Paula," requested Mrs. Doherty in a quiet voice.

Paula did as she was told, stepping barely a foot in front of the mirror. The paper image of Paula suddenly filled with her, with an inch to spare all round.

"Step so close that you're touching the mirror."

Paula did, and realized that the image fit her perfectly. She had become that skinny.

Thursday, December 24, 111 pounds

"I demand to see my daughter!" Emily Romaniuk was used to ordering people around. It alarmed her that the head nurse had refused her permission to see her own daughter. She was the pharmacy manager at this very same hospital, after all. With whom did they think they were dealing?

Nurse Bowley stood her ground. "If you want your daughter to get better, it's important to leave her alone right now."

Emily's eyes widened with anger. "It's Christmas Eve, and my only daughter is in the hospital. Are you implying that my presence would somehow cause my daughter a setback in treatment?"

"Well ... um. That's not exactly what I meant ..." replied Nurse Bowley, her face flushing in embarrassment.

"Then I will see her right now."

Without waiting for a response, Emily Romaniuk strode down the hospital corridor. She pushed open the door to her daughter's room.

She was shocked at the sight that confronted her. When Paula was still at home, she had seemed thin, but now she was truly skeletal. "My God, Paula, what have they done to you?"

"Mom, I've got to get out of this place," said Paula. "I don't want to spend Christmas all by myself," she began. "And besides, if I stay here, I'm going to lose my whole year of school."

Emily looked into her daughter's eyes. "If you came home, you would have to promise to eat properly, dear. You're going to do permanent damage to yourself, the way you're carrying on."

Paula nodded in agreement. "I realize that Mom, and I would have eaten more, but the food is awful here."

Paula knew it was the right thing to say. Emily had never been able to stomach the hospital food in the cafeteria. She could imagine the revulsion her daughter would have towards what they passed off as food in this place. "Let me talk to Doctor Tavish," said Mrs. Romaniuk.

Doctor Tavish was adamant that Paula stay in the hospital. "I'm sure a bed will be opening up soon at Homewood," he pleaded.

"Then she'd be even further away from us at Christmas," replied Mrs. Romaniuk. "We'll see how she does over Christmas at home. If she doesn't gain some weight, we'll reconsider."

Doctor Tavish agreed, however reluctantly.

An hour later, Paula was packed and ready to go. As her mother led her down the hallway and out to the elevators, Paula smiled at the two women who were standing side by side in the nurses' station, pained expressions on their faces.

Paula celebrated her arrival home by eating a generous serving of Christmas cake and a glass of eggnog — in front of her mother — who sipped a diet cola. When she was finished, Paula put down her fork and said, "I'm really tired, Mom. I think I'll lie down."

She grabbed her overnight bag and headed up the stairs. Before she got to her own bedroom, she tapped on Erik's door. "Come in," he called.

She found him at his usual place in front of the computer, *Civilization II* loaded and ready to play. "Do you want to play for a bit, Paula?" he asked, a look of eager expectation on his face.

Paula felt a twinge of guilt. She couldn't play right now, because she had to take some laxatives immediately, or the Christmas cake and eggnog would be there to stay. "Maybe later," she said. "I just wanted to give you your Game Gear back." She handed him the worn lunch bag which was wrapped around his prized possession. "And thanks for being such a great brother."

As he reached up and grabbed the bag, Paula tried to ignore the look of hurt in his eyes. She turned around towards the door. "I tried to stop them, sis, but they wouldn't listen."

Paula frowned at his comment, not understanding what he was referring to. She walked down the hallway to her own bedroom and opened the door.

What a shock!

The beloved oil by Gramma Pauline was gone. And Paula's collection of posters had been removed from the walls and the wallpaper that had brought her joy since childhood had been stripped away. In its place were pale pink walls bordered with English cabbage roses. Her bed and dresser, which had once been dark-stained oak, were now painted a high-gloss white. Paula ran to her dresser and opened the top drawer. The underwear that she had casually tossed in as it was laundered was now folded neatly and stacked in rows. In alarm, she groped with her hand to the back of the drawer. Her laxatives were gone.

"Do you like how we did your room?" Paula's

mother was standing in the doorway regarding her daughter. "Merry Christmas!"

Was her mother crazy? Paula felt defiled. Invaded. Did her mother not realize that this was her room, and that nobody else had the right to be in it, let alone destroy it?

"It's nice, Mom," she said in a flat voice. What was the use after all?

A more immediate concern was that she had capitulated and eaten the food her mother had served her. And here she was without laxatives.

"Mom, would you mind if I went on a walk?"

"But I thought you were tired," said her mother, looking at her suspiciously.

"I am," replied Paula. "But I need some fresh air."

"I see nothing wrong with that, honey. Just don't overdo it.

Paula bundled herself in layers of clothes against the snowy cold, then dashed down the stairs and ran out the door. She jogged through the snow to the old public library. The now vacant century-old building was graced with an austere front and a bank of steps on either side.

"That cake and nog probably contained six hundred calories minimum," considered Paula. "It takes running up and down once to burn ten calories ... so I'll have to run up and down these steps sixty times."

Paula raced up one side of the steps and ran down

the other again and again. She could feel her heart beating and she became light-headed. That probably came from the days of enforced rest at the hospital, she rationalized. Ignoring her fluttering heart, she continued her frenzied pace. All at once, she became unutterably tired. Her breath became so laboured that it was like trying to breathe under water. She stumbled to a sitting position on the bottom step and held her head in her hands.

She began to feel a tingling in her left hand and all the way up her arm. She shook her hand to try to get the numbness to go away, but it had no effect. She was aware of a sharp pain in her chest. Where her breathing was once laboured, it was now impossible. Paula was gripped with fear. What had she done to herself? She was so weak that she didn't even have the strength to sit up. Her body lurched forward and she fell off the step. Gasping for breath, Paula became aware of an even more intense pain radiating throughout her chest.

Paula could feel herself slump into a heap, but she was powerless to recover. Like water draining out of a sieve, her sight slowly began to fade until she could see nothing. With her ability to move gone, and her sight gone, her hearing became more acute. She could hear the muffled thump of a woman in winter boots run toward her, screaming, "Call an ambulance." And then ... nothing. Her hearing was gone. Then the pain left.

Marta

She had the sensation of floating, and she suddenly could see, hear, and feel again, but with an intense, inhuman clarity. She looked down, and observed a heap of clothing lying on the steps, a crowd of strangers gathering around her. She felt nothing but a sense of peace. Where before she had gasped for breath, now she realized that breathing was not necessary.

She was surprised to realize how thin her body had become. It was barely detectable beneath the winter clothes. Maybe what everyone had been telling her was true after all. Her lifeless limbs seemed to have no more substance than the skeleton of the Armenian in the road on that Internet site. What have I done to myself?

As she felt herself rise further, she observed someone administering artificial resuscitation. It amazed her how much she didn't care whether they revived her or not. Down below was the body that had betrayed her. Now she was pure essence.

Then she was engulfed in blackness. Paula groped through the darkness. She was suspended in a miasma of nothingness.

And then the space around her changed. The blackness emitted a metallic glitter, and as Paula watched, it enveloped her in a snaking vertical tunnel. Paula felt trapped. Is this what hell was like?

Then she abruptly became aware of a noxious gush pushing at the soles of her feet and propelling her upwards. She wrinkled her nose as the substance reached her knees and then cried out in horror as it rapidly enveloped her, pushing her up with increasing velocity. And then, the glittering tunnel opened before her to a bright blinding whiteness. She reached toward the light, hoping desperately that there was something solid within it that she could hang onto and pull herself out with. She needn't have bothered. The vile fluid spat her out of the tunnel and splattered around her.

Paula looked around her and saw that she was sitting on what appeared to be the white sand bank of a river. The light she had seen was the reflection of a brilliant sun on glass-still water. She turned to look at the lip of the tunnel which had brought her to this place, but she was just in time to see its glittering blackness close and disappear below the white sand.

Paula wrinkled her nose as she was suddenly aware of a familiar acrid smell. She looked down at her own body and realized with disgust that she was sitting in a pool of vile green curdled fluid. That's what had propelled her to this place! She stood up and tried to brush it from her skin, but to no avail. It was rapidly baking onto her, becoming a part of her skin.

She looked around and noted the barrenness of the place she had come to. There wasn't a stick of vegetation, no ants in the sand, and the water was so still that she knew it held no life.

"I must wash," she decided, and stood up on wobbly legs, taking a step in the direction of the water, but then Paula felt a white-hot light envelop her. She became acutely aware of key incidents in her life. The sensation was like watching a movie while being in the movie.

She saw herself as a baby in her mother's arms and remembered the joy of unconditional love. Family celebrations flashed past, and she re-experienced the thrill of seeing her newborn baby brother for the first time. Images of friends flickered by. And her beloved Gramma Pauline. She had so much to live for.

As quickly as the home movie had started, it was over. Paula took her hands from her eyes and was surprised to see that the pool of vomit had vanished. She held her hands in front of her and noted that they were fresh-scrubbed clean. As was the rest of her body. And then with a gasp, she realized that she was naked.

She heard a rustling behind her, so she crossed her arms in front of her chest in a feeble attempt to hide her nakedness, then turned. Where once there was nothing but sand, now there was a rock. And sitting on the rock was a mirror image of herself. The young woman was dressed in a worn shirt and a pair of baggy pants held up with a leather belt tied tight around her waist. Her feet were bare, except for a few tattered rags, wrapped round and round like bandages.

Like Paula, the vision had long black hair and an angular profile. There was a difference in the eyes, though. This woman's exuded love. She smiled shyly at Paula and extended her hand. Paula took it and was amazed at its warmth and its callused roughness. This was no vision, but a flesh and blood human being. Paula turned the hand knuckle up and noticed another difference between this woman and herself — this woman did not bear the scars of bulimia.

"Who are you?"

"My name is Marta."

Marta stood up and gestured for Paula to approach. And as Paula stepped towards her, she felt a tingling throughout her limbs and a prickly cold feeling at the back of her scalp. Even though they were only inches apart, Marta beckoned her to come closer, and opened her arms as if to embrace. Paula stepped into the mirror image of herself and felt a loving warmth envelop her. "Paula" no longer existed. She had just stepped inside of Marta.

The woman held the back of her hands up to her face and with a shiver of joy, she realized that all the signs of her latest battle had disappeared. Where once there were bruises and needle marks from the nurses' poking and prodding, now there was unblemished, tanned skin. Her hands were callused and dirty with honest hard work, but the knuckles were remarkably smooth. She ran her fingertips lightly over her chest and hips and recognized the contours of her old body.

An overwhelming sense of peace and satisfaction enveloped her. She curled up, hugging her knees with her arms, and fell into a vast, delicious sleep.

April 23, 1915

"Marta, you lazy girl. Wake up!" Marta ignored the voice, content in savouring the satisfying dream. Suddenly, her face and shoulders were covered with a splash of cold water.

"What did you do that for?" she screamed, opening her eyes for the first time, expecting to see her brother, Erik, standing at the foot of her bed. Instead, there was a teenaged girl not much older than herself, holding a dripping earthen jug. Something in the brown eyes and furrowed brow seemed familiar, but Paula couldn't quite place it. The girl was beautiful, however, with finely chiselled features and a birdlike fragility. Her hands seemed familiar, with their long elegant fingers and almond shaped nails.

"You cannot sleep any longer, Marta. The soldiers will be here in an hour and anyone who isn't ready will be shot."

What was this girl talking about? Marta looked around her in dismay. Gone was the white sand and the river. In its place was a dormitory-style room that must have been built for a dozen or more girls. All of the other cots in the room had been stripped of their bedding. A neat stack of rolled bedclothes sat just outside the entranceway of the room.

Marta recognized the gravity of the situation, and while she still didn't quite know what was going on, she remembered this scene with forboding from a dream of the past. Deja vu.

Marta shook the droplets of water from her hair and rolled out of bed. And then, as if she'd done it a thousand times before, she deftly folded up her bedclothes and rolled them into a neat bundle like the other girls in the room must have done.

"When did you change into Kevork's clothing?" asked the older girl.

"What?" Marta asked.

The girl pointed at Marta's shirt and pants. "I knew you were going to try dressing up as a boy, but I didn't think Kevork had given you the clothing yet."

Marta looked down and realized that she was wearing the same shirt and pants that she had worn in her ... dream? Only now, the shirt was clean and white and smelled faintly of soap. Her pants were slightly wrinkled from having been slept in, but they were in good condition, and were held up with a leather belt.

She looked up at the girl and noted that she was wearing an old-fashioned long skirt and a white blouse.

"Get your boots on, grab your bedroll, and let's go find Kevork," the girl said, impatience tingeing her voice.

Marta poked her head underneath her cot and grabbed the pair of boots that she found, suppressing a giggle at the absurdity of it all. She quickly slipped them on and laced them up, then followed the other girl out of the room to meet this Kevork fellow.

Marta looked at her surroundings with dawning familiarity. The dormitory room from which she had exited was part of a huge enclosed city: row upon row of institutional buildings, with a sturdy stone fence built around the whole complex. This was an orphanage, she knew instantly. And she also felt a vague sense of security emanating from the fortress-like walls. This was a place that she wished she never had to leave.

In a flash of insight, she realized that the older girl she was following was her sister, Mariam. She also remembered a brother. She knew that this brother wasn't named Erik.

Mariam led her through the dusty courtyard in the centre of the orphanage complex and then disappeared through the heavy double doors of a one-story oblong building. Without pausing to see whether Marta was following her, Mariam continued down the central corridor, then pulled open the door of one of the rooms at the end.

There sat a a boy ... a young man, really ... on a cot much like the one from which Marta had recently been so unceremoniously awakened. As he looked up and met her eyes, Marta's heart lurched with sorrow, and with love. Like a phrase on the tip of her tongue, she knew he was the love of her life, but for the life of her, she couldn't remember why or how.

He was powerfully built, and over six feet tall, although he still had the eyes of a child. He was dressed in a shirt and pants like Marta's own, and on his feet were heavy boots. He was holding a well-thumbed sheaf of papers in one hand, and nine Turkish gold pounds in the other. His shoulders were hunched over in sadness. Before they had disturbed him, he must have been reading through the letter one last time.

He set the letter down beside him, and Marta craned her neck to read the script. It was not in English, but miraculously, she could read bits and snatches of it — enough to know that his father had died and bequeathed him these coins. She could also read the date on the top sheet — 02/03/1915! Her heart pounded. Nineteen-fifteen was a horrible year. If only she could remember why.

Kevork placed the gold coins on top of the letter. "There are still a few things that we have to do before the Turks return," he said.

Turks?! Fragments of memory flashed before her eyes. She remembered that the last time she saw her parents alive was six years ago. They were in the barley fields. She and Mariam were just little girls then. Her brother ... he had been just two or three. They had left the fields together to play in the city. It was then that the killings had begun. She and Mariam and ... Onnig! Her brother's name was Onnig! They had escaped by laying hidden in silenced horror on the roof of a mosque and watched while the killings happened all around them. Marta could still remember Onnig trying to bite through her fingers as he tried to scream, but she clamped her hand over his mouth to keep him silent.

Others had somehow survived too. Kevork's mother had managed to hide him, but not herself or his baby sister. Where his father was, no one knew.

It was the day of the Adana massacre that Marta met Kevork. He was crazed with grief. And then there was Anna — Kevork's albino aunt. The Turks neither killed nor molested her, so superstitious were they of her appearance.

Anna gathered the children together and they travelled on foot to Marash. Away from the horrors. Away from the memories. Their grandmother took in young Onnig, but she was too poor to keep them all, so Marta and Mariam lived at the orphanage. As did Kevork. Aunt Anna had been hired on as a cook.

"Where's Onnig?" Marta asked.

Mariam and Kevork looked at each other and then at Marta with a pained expression in their eyes. "If only we knew," Mariam replied sadly.

And then Marta remembered more. Just the evening before, she, Mariam, and Kevork had stolen away from the orphanage under the cover of darkness and had travelled on foot through the streets of Marash until they reached the house of Marta and Mariam's grandmother. It was empty, a broken front door creaking on a windless night. Marta could only hope that they had abandoned their home before the soldiers had arrived.

"Sit down, Marta, it's time to cut your hair." Kevork had pulled a pair of scissors from a wooden box at the foot of his bed.

Marta's hands flew up to her head. "Why do you have to cut my hair?"

"What's the matter with you?" Kevork asked wearily. "We've been through this all before. If you want to have the soldiers think you're a boy, you've got to get rid of all that hair."

Marta gulped in dismay. It was apparent that this had been discussed before and she, or whomever she used to be, had agreed. She sat down on the bed beside Kevork, and watched as chunks of her glorious dark hair fell in a pile on the bed.

"You're next," said Kevork, looking at Mariam.

But Mariam was staring at her sister in alarm.

"No," she said. "I'll take my chances as a girl."

Marta looked at her sister and was about to say something, but bit her tongue. Mariam would make a singularly poor boy. Her curves were already too pronounced, and she was far too delicate. Marta was thankful for her heavier build and manly height.

"The coins, Kevork. Would you like me to sew them into your clothing?" Mariam drew a needle and thread from a small pocket in her blouse.

"I think we should each take three," said Kevork. "That way, if we get separated, we'll each have something to live on."

"Fine," said Mariam. And with quick fingers, she deftly stitched three coins each in the seams of their outfits. As she sewed the coins into her own hems, something clattered from her waistband and fell to the floor.

Marta darted over to her sister and picked up the object. It was a tiny, glittering sickle. At the sight of it, Marta remembered. This had been her mother's sickle. A tiny custom-made sickle, sharp as a razor, yet small enough for a delicate woman to handle. She remembered a scene from six years ago — the last time she had seen it in her mother's hands. Marta, her brother, and sister had travelled from Marash on foot all the way to the barley fields surrounding Adana. This was an annual journey and a sure source of cash for the impoverished family. There were still several weeks of the harvest left, and her parents had been in a good mood, anticipating what they could buy when the harvest was done and they returned to their home in Marash.

Parantzim, their mother, had sent the children off to play. And when the children came back to the barley fields hours later, there was only silence. And a bloodstained sickle.

Marta ran her index finger over the sharp inner blade and watched in fascination as a bead of her own blood appeared.

"You'll hurt yourself," said Mariam brusquely, reaching out to her sister and delicately removed the sickle from Marta's grasp. Mariam tucked the treasured object into the back of her belt and then said, "So are we ready?"

"We'd better be," replied Kevork. "The soldiers will be here in minutes."

The three grabbed their bedrolls and headed out to the central courtyard of the orphanage complex.

They were among the last of the orphans to collect in the courtyard. Marta looked around her, and was both surprised and not surprised, when she recognized individual children who had gathered in rows, sitting upon their bedrolls. Paris, a little girl with mischievous eyes and buck teeth smiled broadly as she saw Marta approach. Marta instinctively reached down and lightly patted the girl's shoulder as she walked by.

Altogether, there were about two hundred children sitting patiently for orders. Marta noticed a small group of adults off to one side, their own bedrolls piled in a heap. An animated discussion was taking place, and Marta strained to hear the words.

She recognized Josefine Younger, the German missionary who supervised both the boys' orphanage, Beitshalom, and the girls', Bethel. The woman's greying blonde hair was usually upswept in a tight bun, but today the bun was in disarray. Even her steel glasses were askew. She was talking animatedly to Anna, Kevork's aunt.

With Anna and Miss Younger was Mr. Karellian, the boys' trade teacher, and Tante Maria, the elderly laundress. These three were the only Armenian adults in the complex, and as the voices drifted closer to Marta, she could hear that Miss Younger was arguing furiously with the others, trying to convince them to leave while they still had the chance.

"If we leave," replied Tante Maria in a firm voice. "They may take their anger out on you. Or on the children." The other two nodded in agreement.

Just then, the massive gates of the orphanage complex creaked open and a strikingly handsome Turk on a white stallion sauntered in, followed by soldiers on foot.

This was the infamous Mahmoud Sayyid, the Captain in charge of the Young Turk army in the city of Marash, and the only son of the wealthy Cherif Mahmoud.

He reined his horse inches from Miss Younger's face, then glanced disdainfully at her and her trembling companions. "This cannot be all of your adult Armenians," he said, cracking his whip towards the sorry group.

The rows of children just metres away were so fearful that not a single child took a breath.

"The records show that you have more than a dozen Armenians on staff."

"You are mistaken," replied Miss Younger.

Captain Sayyid dismounted, handing the reins to one of the soldiers. He strutted past the small group of adults and walked over to where the rows of children sat in silence.

He stopped in front of Kevork and stared down at the young man as he sat quietly on his bedroll. Crooking his finger, he beckoned Kevork to stand up. Kevork blushed, then obliged. Even with hunched shoulders, Kevork stood a full head taller than the Captain.

Mahmoud Sayyid flashed an angry look at Miss Younger. "This is no child," he declared. And then with a motion of his finger, he directed Kevork to join the adults.

"He's only fifteen," said Miss Younger.

"I don't believe you," replied the Captain.

Next, he stepped in front of Marta. Her heart was pounding so wildly in her chest that she was sure he could hear it. Would he suspect that she was a girl?

As he did with Kevork, he beckoned her to stand. And like Kevork, she should have towered over the Turk, but she took her chances and crouched slightly, making them the same height. "This one is more man than boy," shouted the Captain. "What tricks are you playing on me, woman?"

"That .... boy ...." she stumbled, "that boy is only thirteen. He's no risk to you."

"Don't tell me my business," replied Mahmoud Sayyid in a quiet angry voice. "If these are children, then you're feeding them too well." He gestured to Marta to stand with Kevork and the adults.

When he stepped in front of Mariam, a smile broke on his face. Brushing the side of her cheek lightly with his hand, he turned to Miss Younger and said, "Where have you been hiding this one?"

Miss Younger's face flushed brightly in alarm, but she remained silent.

He grabbed Mariam's hand and roughly pulled her toward him. "You'll come with me," he said.

She pulled her hand away from his and stepped back. "I will not go."

His smile turned cold as he listened to her

declaration. Without uttering a word, he drew a pistol from his belt and shot Paris, the little girl with the mischievous eyes. Blood splattered from the wound in her neck as she fell back into the arms of the girl sitting behind her. A frightened hush descended upon the courtyard. Miss Younger stepped forward, intending to help the injured girl, but the Captain pointed his pistol menacingly in her direction and said, "Stay where you are, or you will be next."

Paris died before their eyes, but the children surrounding her maintained their grim silence. They watched as the Captain inspected the rest of the children and designated about a dozen in all as "adults."

Mariam stood trembling at the Captain's side as she watched him decide the fate of people she loved. She dared not say a word to him when he was done, but the question remained in her eyes.

"They will die, but you will live," he said. Then he turned to Miss Younger, "I will be back for these adult Armenians at dawn tomorrow." Then he shook his finger at her, "Don't try to trick me, or you'll regret it."

With that, he pushed Mariam onto his horse, then mounted in front of her, and with the soldiers following on foot, he left the compound.

As soon as he was beyond the gates, Miss Younger rushed to the bloodied body that had been Paris. Miss Younger gently picked it up and carried it away.

Deportation

Most everyone had left the central courtyard — the "adults" to tie up the last details of their lives, the children to run off their pent-up energy. Not a few followed Miss Younger.

Marta remained in the courtyard, as did Kevork. Now that they were alone, he clasped her hand in his. "Whatever happens," he said. "We will be together."

Hand in hand, they walked to the spot where the Captain's horse had stood. "Do you think Mariam will get out of this alive?" Marta asked Kevork, kicking the dirt with the tip of her boot, as if by hiding the impressions of the horse's hooves, she could change her sister's fate.

"Mariam's more resilient than she looks," replied Kevork.

That night, as Marta lay in her dormitory bed, her mind jumbled in confusion with all that had happened. Where was her little brother, Onnig? And what about her grandmother? She now also recalled an aunt and cousins. They too had been staying with her grandmother. Had they all been killed, or were they among the first of the Armenians to be exiled from Marash? And Marta was sick with fear over the fate of her sister, Mariam. Should she have insisted that Mariam dress up as a boy, like she had herself? Would Mariam be safer with the Captain, or on the deportation march? These problems spun through Marta's head until the early hours of the morning when she finally fell into an exhausted sleep.

At seven a.m. sharp, Turkish soldiers on horses arrived at the orphanage gates. Each carried a whip. The officer in charge was again Captain Mahmoud Sayyid, who jumped off his horse and looked at the handful of doomed Armenians, each of whom carried their worldly possessions on their backs.

Marta, Kevork and Miss Younger stood nervously beside a wagon, packed to the brim, with a donkey ready to pull it.

"What's in the wagon?" asked Captain Mahmoud Sayyid, strutting in front of them.

"I am sending extra supplies," said Miss Younger.

"That won't be necessary," he said

"... But ..." started Miss Younger.

"Leave it here!"

At this point Mr. Muller, one of the German missionaries, approached Miss Younger and the Captain and asked if he could speak to him "man to man." Miss Younger walked away in frustration. Marta watched the conversation with curiosity and noticed the sunlight gleam on several Turkish gold pounds as they passed from Mr. Muller's hands to the Captain's hands. Then the officer walked away, ignoring the wagon.

The handful of deportees from the orphanage were escorted out the gates with the sobs of anguished teachers and orphans at their backs. By the time they got to the centre of Marash, they were joined by thousands of others.

With the hot sun beating down, the column of deportees slowly snaked its way out the gates of Marash and in the direction of the desert. Marta, in her boy's outfit, kept close to Kevork, and the two of them made an effort to stay towards the end of the column, amidst a cluster of men. Mr. Karellian and Aunt Anna were with them too, but Tante Maria had somehow disappeared from sight. Marta prayed that she had been spirited away by Miss Younger. Marta also prayed for Miriam's survival.

Just in front of them hobbled elderly women and men, and when someone had trouble continuing on, the able-bodied men would take turns assisting them. There was also a cluster of adolescent girls who had somehow been designated as "adults" and sent on this exile. The men tried their best to protect them from the bands of Turkish youths who jeered from the side of the road. Marta saw the humiliation in the faces of the taunted girls and she was grateful not to be one of them.

Soldiers rode up and down the long column with whips that cut at the heels of stragglers, but the pace was tortuously slow, nonetheless. By nightfall, the deportees were only a mile outside the eastern gates of Marash. The soldiers let their prisoners prepare food and settle down to sleep under the stars.

Since they had so recently departed, the stores of food were still plentiful. Marta and Kevork were each issued a small loaf of bread drizzled with olive oil, a few ounces of hard cheese, and a flask of water.

Marta marvelled at the oily bread and was amazed at how hungry the sight of it made her feel. She took a huge bite and relished in the sensation of olive oil dripping down her chin. She ate every last crumb of bread and every bit of cheese with a vague sense of triumph. The Turks may wish us to die, she thought, but I'm not about to co-operate.

The next morning, one of the women complained that her legs hurt and she couldn't walk. Aunt Anna tried to pull the woman to her feet, but she just sat back down on the ground, refusing to budge. A soldier who couldn't have been any more than seventeen was passing by. "Get that woman on her feet!" he screamed. Anna looked up at him. "You're Armenian," she said. "What are you doing fighting with the Turks?" The young soldier paled.

Just then, Captain Mahmoud Sayyid came riding by. He looked at Anna, and then at the woman.

"I'll get her to move for you," he said, flicking the whip across the woman's face. The other deportees hurried by the scene, averting their eyes. The woman who had been whipped slumped down onto the roadside. With quiet dignity, she looked into the eyes of her tormentor. "Kill me now, if you must," she challenged.

Anna tried to pull her to her feet, but she refused to move. Another soldier passed by. He surveyed the scene, then casually took out his gun and shot the woman in the chest. She fell back, dead.

The other deportees who were still forming the column close by, turned their heads away and walked on. Anna, who was spattered with the woman's blood, had slumped down to the ground in a faint. The Armenian soldier got off his horse, picked her up, and hoisted her across his saddle like a sack. The body of the woman was left where it was a warning to all who would be tardy.

Each day of marching was like the last. Every day, a few more people would refuse to go further, and they were either left at the side of the road to fend for themselves in the wilderness, or they were shot.

Marta, still dressed as a boy, was thankful that she blended in. Aside from her, there were a few other girls dressed as boys, and Anna, whose strange paleness repelled the soldiers. All of the other females left in the column were children and grandmothers.

As the days wore on, the column of deportees inched closer to the heat of the desert. Each day, the stores of food became scarcer, as did the water. Marta was grateful for the Turkish gold pounds sewn into her clothing. She traded one of the coins for a leather pouch filled with raisins and a flask of water. She supplemented her daily ration of a stale piece of mouldy bread and a cup of water with her own life-saving supply of nourishment.

Anna and Mr. Karellian walked at the end of the column, keeping their eyes open for stray children. Once, while the group was resting at the end of a gruelling day, a Turkish woman came by, inspecting the children, looking for a suitable boy. She spotted a relatively healthy four-year-old and squatted by his side.

"Would you like to be my son?" she asked, handing the boy a cup of water. He drank it greedily. Anna walked over to the woman. "You Turks belong in hell," she said. The woman looked up sadly. She paused, looked back at the little boy and said, "I can't change the world, but I can save a little boy."

The child wanted to go with the woman, so Anna shrugged her shoulders and called after him, "Go! But always remember: you are Armenian."

One day, the gendarmes ordered the deportees to divide into two groups. One was for all the married people, the other, all the single. Questions buzzed up and down the column. What would be better? To be married or single?

"Maybe they're going to make sure all the married couples will be deported with each other," suggested

Marta hopefully. "We should pretend to be married."

"Or maybe they're going to kill all the married couples," Kevork countered.

All around them, people were frantically looking for "husbands" and "wives" so that they could go stand in the married group.

"Marta," Kevork said. "Let us not make a mockery of our love. We should stand with the singles group."

Marta was not happy with this suggestion, but she didn't argue. The group of married people was about triple the size of the singles group. Anna and Mr. Karellian, who could have easily posed as a couple, were also standing in the singles group.

The gendarmes came over and ordered the married group to march over a huge sand dune to the left, and the singles were ordered to keep marching along the road to the right. Moments later, Marta heard muffled screams. All in the married group were bludgeoned with hatchets and clubs. No need to waste bullets.

As the days passed, the sun beat down and the air was unbearably hot. Water and food were scarce. The bedraggled column of deportees was being marched into the heart of the desert.

Daily rations no longer existed. Marta watched as one woman in her group resorted to eating tufts of grass that grew in patches all over the desert. She watched with despair, when later the same day, the woman curled into a ball of agony and died from the toxic effects of the grass. There was no food to be had, and no food to be bought.

Marta watched with fascination a certain man who would follow behind one of the soldier's horses. When the horse defecated, he would fall to his knees and pick through the droppings for a stray kernel of undigested corn. The man lived, while others around him died.

They were marched to Tel Abiad, a community on the banks of the Euphrates River, south of Urfa. Thousands upon thousands of men, women, and children, half-starved, with blistered feet and open sores showing through their rags, had been gathered together.

The sight of the eerily still blue water made Marta gasp. This was the same river she had seen in her vision. She looked down at the clothes that she was wearing and nodded in understanding. Her shirt was now tattered and nondescript, as were her pants. She had come back to where she had started. There was one difference — on her feet were boots. The sand she had been walking on had worn the soles down to the thickness of a wafer, but they still protected her feet.

"Water," muttered Kevork, as he gazed longingly at the still blueness. He was about to break forward and run from the column, risking the whips and bayonets of the gendarmes, but Marta grasped his arm.

"That water is death," she warned.

Kevork shrugged her hand off his arm and was about to step forward when they were both distracted by cries coming from the the river. On the banks were half a dozen Armenians who'd had the same idea as Kevork. They had drunk their fill of salt water. Stomachs distended with malnutrition and dehydration now burst like rotting fruit. They died an agonizing death as the gendarmes looked on, grateful that they didn't have to waste more bullets.

One day, Kevork pointed to a man in a tattered group of deportees resting on the side of the road, "Does he look familiar?"

"No," said Marta. "Who do you think it is?"

"I am sure that is the Vartabed Garabed."

A "Vartabed" was an Armenian priest. And when Anna had first led her group of orphans back to Marash from Adana, her first stop had been to the Vartabed's residence. In his kindness, he had arranged for Kevork, Marta, and Mariam to be admitted to the orphanage, and he had asked Miss Younger to hire Anna as a cook. Onnig, who had been very young at the time, had refused to leave his aunt and grandmother to go to the orphanage with his sisters, and thus the family had been further fragmented.

"God Bless you, Very Reverend Father," Kevork said, kneeling in front of the startled priest. Marta got on her knees beside Kevork and bent her head in humility.

"You look familiar .... yes ..... I know ...... you two are Adana survivors," exclaimed Vartabed Garabed. "You were living at the orphanage ... correct?"

"Yes," Marta replied, trying hard not to show the pity she felt for the priest. While Marta and Kevork had been able to scavenge bits of food, it was obvious that the priest had not eaten for some time. He had wasted away so dramatically that it was a miracle he could still live. Marta had an urge to force him to eat. She felt around in her pocket and pulled out a few dried raisins, left over from her bag.

"Vartabed Garebed, please take this." She placed the raisins in the priest's hand. Father Garabed looked down at the precious food as if he didn't recognize what it was. Marta felt liking shaking him.

"When were you deported?" asked Kevork.

"My parish was one of the last groups to leave Marash," replied the priest, still staring absently at the raisins.

"Do you know what happened to the Hovsepian family?" asked Marta.

"Your aunt ... and her children ... and your grandmother ... correct?"

"And my baby brother, Onnig," added Marta.

"Three children, that's right." The priest absent-mindedly picked up the raisins one by one, but didn't eat them, and then said, "I heard that the three children were taken in by a Moslem family in

Marash to be raised as Turks. Nobody knows what happened to your aunt or grandmother. They were not with the others when that area was rounded up."

"Do you think they might be in hiding?" Kevork asked.

"Where would they hide?" asked the priest.

Escape

Every day, soldiers chose a group of deportees and took them away. Mr. Karellian was among the first of their friends to be dispatched. Nobody ever came back. And Marta and Kevork could only guess what happened to them. Each day, new deportees arrived to take their place.

Now that they were no longer in transit, groups of Kurds congregated on the outskirts of the transshipment area, risking the wrath of the soldiers in hopes of making a bit of money by selling food to the deportees. Both Kevork and Marta still had coins sewn into their clothing. The Kurds were happy to exchange food and local currency for a piece of Kevork's gold.

Marta savoured every bite of mouldy bread and every shrivelled olive. She watched with dismay as her once strong and healthy body withered and contracted. But she would not let the Turks win. She was determined to live.

Marta and Kevork separated themselves from the Marash deportees and made a point of blending in with the newest set of arrivals each day. Anna still walked behind the last stragglers in the column, ensuring that they didn't get lost. Nobody knew what she managed to eat, but she refused all the food that Marta and Kevork offered her. They kept the Vartabed Garabed with them, and shared with the priest any food they could find. But Marta saw him giving away every precious morsel.

The three of them lay low, but they could only delay their fate for so long.

One morning, Marta woke up with the sharp realization that her precious boots were gone. Kevork's were also gone. As they had slept through the night, a band of Kurds had stealthily come by, removing all in sight that was of value.

Marta watched as Kevork walked over to the corpse of an elderly Armenian who had died during the night. Gently, he removed the man's shirt, and as he walked back to where Marta was sitting, he tore the shirt into strips and handed half of them to her. "Wrap these around your feet," he said.

When Marta was finished, she looked down at her feet as a well of apprehension rose up in her throat. With the dirty rags twisted round and round her feet, her outfit was now exactly as it had been in her dream. She looked around at the malnourished group of deportees who had somehow still managed to survive.

Kevork still sat beside her, wrapping his feet in the rags, when a soldier came up to him and poked him with a bayonet.

"You're still here?" the gendarme remarked in surprise. "Get over with that group!"

Kevork got to his feet and stumbled over to the newest doomed mass of humanity.

Marta got up and followed him. "Go away!" Kevork hissed.

"I go where you go."

"You! Get back with the others!" As the gendarme grabbed Marta by the shirt to pull her away, it tore, exposing creamy white skin.

"Hey! You're a girl! I thought all the girls were gone by now!" The soldier grabbed Marta's arm and she cried out in pain. Kevork pushed away the restraining arms of the gendarme and ran toward Marta, but another gendarme noticed and stuck out his foot, tripping him. That man held a bayonet at Kevork's back. "Move and you're dead."

The soldier who held Marta called out, "Friends! I've got a girl here!

Just then, Anna came from out of nowhere. She grabbed a bayonet from a nearby soldier's belt and lunged at the man who was holding Marta. He saw her coming and ducked in the nick of time. Then the guards and deportees watched in horror as Anna lunged again, this time stabbing Captain Mahmoud Sayyid in the neck. Time stood still. Soldiers and deportees alike stared as the man collapsed, blood soaking the white of his uniform. Anna stood defiantly beside him, the bayonet with its bloodied blade still gripped in her hands. The soldier who was holding on to Marta was as mesmerized by the scene as everyone else.

"RUN!" shouted Anna, breaking the spell. Marta pulled away from her captor just as his grip was regaining its strength. She dashed into the crowd.

The man's attention was now directed at Anna. "Infidel!" And with one swift movement he pierced Anna's heart with his bayonet.

Then the soldier turned to deal with Marta. But she had vanished. The other prisoners had quickly closed their ranks upon her, hiding her from the soldier's sight. The soldier grabbed the Vartabed Garabed by his twig-thin arm and marched him over to Kevork's doomed group. "You can pay for that girl's insolence."

Marta watched helplessly from her hiding place as Kevork and the priest and ten other men were packed into a wooden dinghy and pushed out onto the Euphrates. They were being taken yet deeper into the desert.

Marta choked back tears as she watched her beloved Kevork disappear over the horizon. For just one moment, she hesitated. What was the point of even trying to escape? They would catch up with her sooner or later and she would die like everyone else.

But she had no illusions about what would happen to her if the soldiers found her. And she did not plan on letting that happen. She lay low, hiding among the deportees until night. The emaciated group had fallen into an exhausted sleep, but most of the soldiers stayed up to drink and play cards. Marta waited until the wee hours of the morning when the soldiers had drifted off to sleep too. Even the gendarme who was supposed to be keeping the night watch had fallen into a deep sleep. After all, where could these people possibly go?

Marta gazed at the hilly areas in the distance.

Quietly, she picked her way through the mass of inert bodies. Marta was at the very edge of the encampment. Just a few more steps ...

"Halt! Who goes there?"

It was the same young soldier who had started this journey with the orphanage contingent.

"You're the traitor Armenian," Marta said boldly.

"Don't say that!" he responded, stepping back hesitantly. "I've become a Moslem."

"Hypocrite."

"I could kill you," said the youth.

"Go ahead."

The boy did nothing. The two Armenians glared at each other. Then Marta walked fearlessly out of the encampment in full view of the young soldier. She knew that he was watching her, but he did not shoot.

She headed for the hills by the light of a new moon. She found several caves, all of good size. But there was a problem. Deportees before her had also found this hiding place, and the caves were full of death. Marta thought of her own parents rotting in a cave in Adana.

But there was nowhere else to hide. She had to distance herself from exactly who it was that she was stepping over as she made her way to the mouth of one of the caves. As the stench of rotting bodies wafted around her, she looked up at the night sky and focused on the moon. She straightened her back and tried to breathe in a bit of the air above the stench. She took one huge last gulp, then ducked down, into the cave, amidst the corpses. A deep blackness enveloped her. Marta held her breath as long as she could and tried to use her hands as eyes as she entered ever deeper into the cave. Her hands touched paper-thin flesh cold on the bone. She tried not to think of the hands that had caressed babies, and the feet that had walked miles in the desert in hope of life, but ending up here. Through the blackness, she imagined hundreds of dead eyes staring up at her. Yet she wasn't afraid. She crawled deeper into the cave, through openings so small that no well-fed soldier would be able to enter. No one else had penetrated the cave as deeply as she. Marta was alone. Her place of refuge was a cavity in which she could not sit up nor stretch out her legs. She curled herself like a baby in the womb and fell asleep.

Marta dreamt that she was hovering above herself, watching the body of Marta sleep amidst the dead. She thrashed about, but kept on hitting her arms against the walls. She woke up to the sound of someone screaming. It took her a moment to realize that they were her own screams. She shuddered, and fell into a deep, dreamless sleep.

She woke again. Had hours passed? Or even days? Marta didn't know. Her throat was parchment dry.

Suddenly, she could hear screaming, and this time it wasn't her own. She held her breath and listened. Not just screaming, but voices too. Coming from the mouth of the cave. She could hear one loud voice. It sounded like an auctioneer —

"... who'll give me a gold pound for this one? Two? Yes ... you! How about three ... anybody for three?"

She recognized the voice. It was one of the gendarmes. Marta was paralyzed with fear. "But they can't reach me all the way in here," she reminded herself. Her heart was beating so hard that she was sure the people at the mouth of the cave could hear it.

The "auction" went on for what seemed like an eternity. While Marta was safe in the womb of the cave, she listened in despair as other women suffered a fate that could be her own any day. When the auction finally ended and the crowd dispersed Marta was struck by the sudden thundering silence. The sounds of weeping and groaning had become the norm since the deportations. Now she was enveloped in a cold timeless death.

It wasn't the stench of the cave that made her finally leave. The smell of death had become all too common for that. It was that she would starve if she stayed any longer, but there was a slim chance of survival if she emerged. Marta crept towards the entrance of the cave, past the heaps of corpses. When she reached the entrance, she tried to stand up, but wobbled like a newborn. She sat back down and looked around.

The black of night was almost bright compared to the darkness of the cave. Marta could see the outlines of the deportation encampment in the distance, and the shimmering seduction of the Euphrates just beyond.

She looked longingly at the river, but she had seen what death by salt water looked like.

Marta's legs were so weak that she could not stand up. How could she get away from this place if she couldn't even get onto her feet? She dragged herself along the ground and searched through the clothing of the bodies closest to the mouth of the cave. She didn't quite know what she was looking for — there was so much she needed after all. Marta removed a tattered cloak from the corpse of an old man and wrapped it around her body for warmth, oblivious of its scent of death. What she needed more than anything was water. She found a cane under the body of a woman who was still clutching the remains of her newborn infant. And then a miracle! A tiny bit of brackish water in a skin container around the mother's waist. Marta drank it up greedily. The sensation of the drops of water on her parched tongue brought untold joy to her heart. She would not let the Turks win. She was determined to live in spite of them. She fastened the empty skin at her waist, and slowly, painfully, hobbled on. As she carefully picked her way through the corpses, she spied a heel of dry bread on the ground. She picked it up and pressed it to her chest, so thankful was she for this tiny bit of nourishment. As she was about to bite into it, her eyes focused on the tiny tooth marks of its former owner. She looked down by the ground and realized that it had fallen from the hand of a boy who had died within his mother's embrace. Mother and son both looked surprisingly peaceful in death. His shaggy black hair was grimed with dust, and in the moonlight, just for a moment, it reminded Marta of Erik's sandy blonde hair. She gasped in sorrow.

I will not let them win, she vowed. Then she broke off a small chunk of the bread and forced it onto her swollen tongue — as much a sacrament as nourishment.

She needed to find another hiding place before dawn. The soldiers and neighbouring villagers were always on the lookout for runaways. And if Marta were found, death was the least of her worries.

Leaning heavily on the cane, she hobbled along, keeping clear of the road. She would look ahead and determine a place to try for — a stray bale of hay, a bush, or a shack. Then she would shuffle quickly over to that object and collapse. This procedure was repeated again and again. Marta had managed to get a mile or so away from the cave and the deportation encampment when the first glimmers of dawn appeared over the horizon. She knew that she was far from safe. She spied a wagon about a quarter of a mile up ahead. It was filled with something, she didn't know what. Should she try to get there before the dawn gave her away? What choice did she have?

It took all of her energy to get to the wagon. She looked inside. It was filled with a variety of personal items — clothing, baskets, worn boots, stolen from dead and not-so-dead Armenians. She awkwardly climbed into the cart, burrowing down under as far as she could, and promptly fell asleep.

Saad

Marta woke up with a start. The wagon was moving. Where it was going was not so important at this point — as long as it was away. Marta could hear the driver talking — an elderly man speaking Turkish. Every once in a while a youthful voice would answer. The rhythmic motion of the moving wagon, and the warmth of the items on top of her combined to make it impossible for her to stay awake. She drifted off, dreaming that Kevork was holding her in his arms, rocking her gently.

When Marta finally did wake up, it was because the cart had stopped moving. Marta was chilly. She drew her cloak tightly around her shoulders. Did that mean it was night time? Maybe the driver had stopped somewhere for the night. Her mouth was dry like the desert sand. Her tongue had cracked, and her lips were covered with sores. Should she risk looking to see where she was? If she stayed hidden in the wagon too long she was bound to be discovered. Besides, she had to find food and water.

Slowly, and quietly, Marta burrowed her way to the top of the items in the wagon. She looked around. They were in a tiny hamlet and it was dark. The horses had been stabled, but the cart had been left in the open in front of a public house just as it had been when she had crawled into it. As she took in her surroundings, Marta was startled by a pair of eyes staring in at her from the passenger seat of the wagon.

"You're one of those Armenians, aren't you?" Her heart pounded in fear. The voice was that of the Turkish driver's youthful companion.

"What are you doing out so late at night?" Marta asked, surprised at her bravado.

The boy was taken aback. "I ... I ... couldn't sleep." Then he said, "it isn't me who has to explain anything. You're the one hiding in somebody else's wagon."

"Please don't tell your grandfather that you've seen me," she pleaded.

"He's my uncle," replied the boy. "And why shouldn't I tell him?"

"Do you know what will happen to me if I'm found?"

"You'll be deported, just like all the other Armenian swine."

"And I'll die."

"Then you must deserve to die," the youth replied.

Marta noticed a silhouette at the door to the little inn. She ducked. "What are you doing out here, Saad my boy? It was the voice of the driver.

"Nothing, uncle. I couldn't get to sleep so I came out here for some air."

"But I heard voices," the man persisted.

"That was just me talking to myself."

"Well get in here and go to sleep. We've got a long drive ahead of us tomorrow."

The boy was gone. Marta's heart raced. He had covered up for her.

"Pssst! You in there, wake up." It was Saad's voice. Marta burrowed her head out. He was alone. "Here is some bread and milk." He handed it to her and watched sullenly as she tried to drink the milk. She was extraordinarily thirsty, but her lips and tongue were so parched and swollen that she couldn't seem to navigate the earthen mug of milk. This food was so precious to her, but her body refused to take it in. As she dribbled more milk down the front of her shirt than down her throat, she groaned in despair. Saad reached forward and broke off a bit of bread, dipped it in the milk, and handed it to her. "Here," he said. "This should make it easier."

"Thank you," Marta said solemnly, looking into Saad's brown eyes.

"Don't think I'm going to help you for nothing," the boy said. "You'll have to pay me."

"I will," replied Marta. She thought of the two remaining gold pounds from Kevork that were sewn safely in her seams. She reluctantly drew out one and handed it to him.

"Is this all you have?" ask Saad, turning the coin over in his hand.

Marta hesitated. She desperately wanted to keep the last coin, because her journey was far from over. But it would take nothing for Saad to catch her in a lie, and to anger him meant certain death. "I have one more coin," she replied.

"I'll take it too," he said, holding out his hand.

Marta reluctantly gave it to him. Saad grinned with delight, and put both coins in his pocket. Then he walked back into the inn.

An hour or so later, Saad and his uncle got back into the wagon and continued their journey. As the cart rocked back and forth, the milk and bread that had so soothed Marta's parched mouth now sloshed perilously in her stomach. Adding to her distress was the stuffy warmth of her hiding place. While her sojourn in the cave had been confining, this was smothering. Quietly, she burrowed through the piles of shoes and clothing and worn household goods until her hand touched the wooden slat at the back of the cart. Then, with the wood at her back as her guide, she slowly inched her way into an upright position, pulling away items from the top of her head as it broke the surface. She drank in a huge gulp of fresh air and revelled in the bit of breeze as it tousled the short hairs on the top of her head. From this position, she could clearly see the brightly coloured cloth that was wrapped around the driver's head. If he turned around this moment, he would see her. Marta untangled a grey cotton shirt from the topmost layer of the pile and placed it over her head, covering the view completely from the front, yet still letting in a welcome breeze at the sides.

Bits of conversation between Saad and his uncle drifted back to her. She learned that they were taking their booty all the way home to Aintab, which was just a week's walk from Marash. If Saad would keep her secret, there was a chance that she would make it back to the orphanage alive.

As the wagon continued on its bumpy ride, Marta realized that she desperately had to attend to some personal needs — but just how does one surreptitiously pee in a wagon? The urgency of the situation increasing every minute, Marta burrowed back down to the bottom of the wagon. Her hands darted back and forth on the planks of wood that made up the bottom platform, searching for gap or a hole. The floor was unfortunately thick and solid and Marta was near desperation when she pulled at a plank of wood that came free in her hand. With relief, she positioned herself over the opening and emptied her bladder, watching as the contents spilled onto the dusty road below. She could only hope that neither Saad nor his uncle would turn and notice the streak of wet on the road.

The next night, when the wagon was tied up to the front of yet another small inn, Saad came out with a loaf of bread, a handful of olives, and a pitcher of water. He watched Marta curiously as she ate. "You look like a skeleton," he said.

But she was alive! The Turks were not going to win this time. She dunked her bread in the water to soften it up and popped it into her mouth gratefully. Never had food tasted so good.

Several nights passed uneventfully, with Saad bringing her food, then staring at Marta as she ate. One night he came empty-handed, "Pay me first."

"I have no more money," responded Marta.

"You are a lying Armenian pig. You people always have more money."

"Honestly, Saad. I have no more money. Check for yourself." And Marta stood up, turning her pockets inside out.

Saad stepped forward and carefully ran his fingers over every seam in her ragged outfit. When his search proved fruitless, he frowned and said, "I'm not keeping you for nothing. Maybe I should just tell my uncle about you now!" This last was said a bit too loudly.

"Tell your uncle what?" The uncle was standing at the door in his nightclothes, hands on hips.

Marta quickly ducked back into the cart and covered herself.

"Nothing uncle."

"Liar," muttered the uncle as he came out to investigate. "You were talking to someone in the wagon. What is going on?"

Marta had ducked to the bottom of the junk by this time and was trembling in fear.

"Get me the pitchfork. You're hiding an Armenian, aren't you?"

Marta could hear Saad's shuffling footsteps.

"Here," he said to his uncle nervously. "But you're wasting your time."

The uncle climbed up to the driver's seat of the wagon and leaned over the pile of rags. With tremendous force, he pushed the pitchfork into the deepest part of the pile. He missed Marta's head by an inch. She could hear him curse as he tried to pull the pitchfork free of shoes and clothing. Marta used the opportunity to pull herself over to the loose plank that had served as a toilet, and with her heart pounding in her throat, she lowered herself down through the opening and clung to the axle before the weapon could come down a second time. The man poked every spot of the wagon load as Marta clung in terror underneath.

"I guess you can stop talking to the wagon now, boy," chuckled the uncle maliciously as he walked back to the inn.

"Are you all right?" called Saad tremulously.

Marta shook with fear as she gripped onto the axle. She did not answer.

"He killed her," cried Saad as he stumbled back to the inn.

Marta dropped down onto the dusty laneway in exhaustion. Her hands were blistered from gripping the axle with such force. She knew she had to get away from the wagon quickly, but there was no place to hide. The area had no trees large enough to hide behind, and the dwellings were few and far between. There was only one place to go — onto the roof of the inn. Marta scrambled up as quietly as she could, then lay flat, trembling with fear.

Early the next morning, Marta watched from her rooftop abode as Saad went to the wagon and feverishly threw items out of it onto the ground. He shook his head in confusion as he got to the bottom and still hadn't found Marta's dead body. That's when he noticed the missing plank. Crouching under the wagon, he traced an outline of Marta's rag-bound footsteps and then looked in the direction it pointed. The inn.

He followed her steps to the inn, and Marta lay frozen on her belly in fear as he climbed onto the roof.

He crouched down beside her and looked her in the eye. "You told me the truth about your money," he said. And then he reached into his pocket and drew out both of Marta's gold coins. "We can each have one."

Marta was stunned by this unexpected generosity. She took the coin, then leaned forward and gently kissed Saad on the cheek. "Thank you," she said.

Saad smiled. Then he got up and left.

She heard the wheels of the wagon creak away some hours later, yet she still stayed on the roof, afraid to come down in the daylight. Once night fell, Marta waited for the noises of the inn to subside, and then climbed down. She ran down the road to Aintab, putting as much distance between her and the inn as she could.

Keeping the road in sight while remaining unseen was difficult, but Marta managed to get to Aintab in four days. She stayed hidden at the outskirts of the city until it was night and then crept in. She walked up and down the still streets, sure that even the soft rhythm of her rag-bound feet was loud amidst such silence. She walked for hours. Then, as the first rays of morning were lighting up the streets, she spied the distinctive silhouette of an Armenian church. At the top of its tall cone-like dome, a crucifix stood out in sharp relief against the dawn. The door opened a crack as she pushed on it. Marta looked in — empty. And looted.

She stepped through the threshold and was instantly enveloped in a vast coolness. Bits of dawn shone through the shattered windows and she could make out the familiar cross-like shape of the stone interior. In spite of the shards of glass that littered the floor, Marta felt safe.

She gingerly picked up bits of glass and set them to one side, and then cleared away torn prayer books and rags and other bits of dirt. When she was finished, there was a clean space large enough for her to lie down in. She curled into a ball and covered herself with the cloak. She fell into a vast sleep, her cheek pressed against the cool stone floor.

She dreamt that she was floating above herself, hovering beneath the arches that held up the dome of the church. She looked down at the tiny form that was Marta, huddled amidst the shattered debris. It wasn't loss that she felt at the sight, though. It was triumph. Her heart beat strongly in a body that wouldn't surrender.

Adila

She woke up with a start when someone's foot crashed into her spine. Peeking out from under her cloak, she saw a woman covered from head to toe in black. Her work-worn hands were massaging a sore shin. Marta could hear her muttering away to herself in Armenian. Armenian?

"Excuse me, *Mairig*," Marta said excitedly, as she sat up, the cloak falling away from her shoulders.

"Ahhhh, it's a ghost," the woman screamed.

"I'm not a ghost, I'm an Armenian girl."

The woman, who was still gasping for air, said nothing.

The old woman was indeed an Armenian, but she had lived in a Turkish harem in Aintab for decades.

"Please help me," Marta begged.

She took the veil from her face and squinted her eyes at Marta. The woman was not as old as Marta had thought, perhaps only forty. She wrung her hands together nervously, as if fighting an inward battle. "I must help you," the woman murmured more to herself than to Marta. "Could God forgive me otherwise?"

She advised Marta to cover herself and wait. She hurried out the door muttering, "What will I do with her? What will I do with her?"

Marta waited. The woman did not come back that day. Marta was hungry and her bladder was full, but she dared not move.

At mid-morning the next day, the woman came back. She lifted her skirts and took out a chador, identical to the black garment she herself was wearing. When she removed her veil, Marta realized that the woman's face was freshly bruised.

"I told my husband that my sister's daughter has come to stay with us. He wasn't happy, but how could he refuse to help family?"

The woman's Moslem name was Adila, changed from her birth name of Anah when she was kidnapped. She never used her husband's actual name. He was simply, "my husband."

Marta had heard quite a bit about Turkish harems,

so she was quite shocked to see Adila's abode. The house was in the poorest part of Aintab, and was nothing more than a glorified mud shack. There was a hallway of about six feet wide by six feet long which entered into the men's living quarters, or *salemlik*. This was perhaps twelve feet square. The only furniture in this room was a built-in sofa made of dry hardened mud protruding from the wall. The floor was covered with brightly coloured carpets.

The *haremlik*, or women's quarters, was the back portion of the room divided off with a single sheet of cloth. Though Adila shared this portion of a room with another woman, it was much smaller than the *salemlik*. It featured no built-in sofa; the women slept on the carpeted floor. Beyond the *haremlik* were two small rooms. One was the bathroom — no more than a hole in the ground and a pail of water. The other room was the "shower" a small cubicle furnished with an upper ledge holding pail equipped with a spigot.

The other woman was older than Adila by a decade, and Turkish by birth. The "first wife" ruled Adila. This wife, known as Idris, was not happy with Marta's arrival.

"The last thing this house needs is another female," she said.

Adila was anxious to get her new charge cleaned up before her husband returned home for the evening meal, so she hurried Marta off to the public baths down the street.

A flurry of memory came to Marta as she stepped through the doors at the *hamam.* How long had it been since she had been clean? At the orphanage, the children would be taken to the public baths once a week. The girls' time was Tuesday morning, and she always looked forward to it. She also remembered the many baths that she had taken with her mother and sister. If only she knew where Mariam was now. Was she still alive? Marta had a feeling that she was. An image of Onnig flashed through her mind too. Her little brother had been too young to bathe with the men, and he considered it quite a treat to splash around in the warm pool, playing with the other children.

"Remove your clothing, please." Marta was startled out of her reveries. An enormously fat bath attendant who was naked, save for a towel around her ample middle, stood beside her. She tried to hide a look of distaste as she regarded Marta's attire. Marta undid her tattered cloak and handed it to the attendant, who wrinkled her nose and held it away from her body with a finger and thumb. "You can put your clothing here," she said, placing the cloak in a pile on the floor, far away from the other bathers' bundles.

Marta sat down on the stone ledge in her open cubicle and slowly began to unwind the rags that bound her feet. They were encrusted with layers of dirt and her heels and toes were covered with calluses. She set the rags down beside her on the ledge, then unbuttoned what was left of her shirt. She rolled the shirt and rags into a bundle and placed them on top of the cloak. She untied her leather belt and her men's trousers dropped to the ground. Marta looked down and gasped at the sight of sharp hip bones nearly protruding from her skin. She placed her hands on her hip bones and carefully traced upwards towards her chest. Each rib bulged against a thin layer of skin. Where breasts should have been was nothing but skin-covered bone. Her pants went into the same pile of rags.

The attendant handed her a pair of *pattens* — the wooden sandals on a platform sole that bath goers wore to keep their feet away from the slippery wet floors.

"Follow me," the attendant said, leading Marta to a small room with a stone platform in the middle. The attendant laid a towel on the platform and Marta lay down on it. The woman threw pails of hot water over Marta, soaking her thoroughly, then she threw a few cups of cold soapy liquid onto her and began to scrub her vigorously with a loofah. Marta obediently turned this way and that, while the woman pummelled away the months of dirt with the soapy foam. Shampoo was lathered into her hair, and Marta felt scabs and dead bugs worked loose and washed away. More pails of hot water were thrown onto her, and then pails of cold water. Marta watched a dirty stream of soapy water splash off the platform and down to the drain below. When she was finished, the woman led Marta to the communal area — a huge stone pool of steaming water. Adila was already there with a towels wrapped around her. Her shoulders relaxed noticeably when she saw Marta, looking clean and almost human, walk into the room. Marta stepped into the warm pool and plunged down, ducking her head under. It felt so good to be clean again. She quickly came up for air and hoisted herself onto the side of the pool beside Adila, who handed her towels to dry and cover herself with.

Adila then gave her an embroidered bag filled with clothing. "Put these on," she said, "and put your rags into this bag so we can burn them at home."

Marta went back to her cubicle and pulled out a light cotton outfit of the sort that Turkish women wore. It consisted of a pair of baggy striped trousers, a plain long-sleeved shift that reached almost down to the hem of the trousers, and a long loose vest to go over that. She pulled out a worn pair of women's cloth shoes and put them on. It felt so good to be in clean clothing again. And the outfit was surprisingly cool and comfortable. She looked at herself in the little wood-framed mirror that was also in the bag. It was too small to see all of her, but what she saw was not Marta, but a fragments of a strange thin Turkish woman. She held the mirror up to her face and saw that her hair had begun to grow back. Now that it was clean, she could see that it was almost chin-length. The eyes were Marta's, although the hollow hungry cheeks belonged to someone else.

Over the indoor clothing went the black hooded chador. She waited at the exit as Adila paid for them both.

When they got home, Adila threw the bundle of Marta's rags into the fire before Marta could tell her about her hidden coin. Marta poked around in the ashes with a twig and found it. Adila wanted her to give it to her for safekeeping, but Marta was desperate to keep this last coin close. So with a mallet and nail, Adila pierced a hole through the centre of the last gold coin and slipped it onto a thin strip of leather.

"Wear it around your neck and out of sight," she said.

Marta was cleanly dressed and presentable by the time the husband came home from his stall in the market.

"So this is your 'niece,'" he said, amused eyes looking at Marta. "I don't notice much family resemblance, but we can use an extra pair of hands."

Idris also realized that Marta was not Adila's niece. She let her know, with a hard look in her eyes, that if Marta were any trouble at all she would be reported in an instant. Marta was expected to do the bulk of household chores, and the numbing routine was repeated without end.

She was the first one up each day. Before the sun rose, Marta would knead the dough for the daily bread, then set it aside in a covered bowl in a warm place outside. Then she would sweep out the hearth, saving any live cinders to light the outdoor oven, and then sweep out the rest of the little hut. She would prepare the Turkish coffee just as the others would begin to waken. The husband would lay down his prayer mat facing Mecca, and say his morning prayers. Then Idris would bustle in to pour him his coffee and glare at Marta to get moving on the bread. It was always a rush to get the first batch of bread ready before the husband asked for it.

There was a small wooden table with a smooth flat surface that Marta used for shaping the bread. Quickly, she would take a handful of the dough and pound it into a smooth round circle. The oven, which had been heating since dawn, would be opened, and she would put in the first piece of dough on a metal sheet with a long handle. Within minutes, the first pita would be ready. Idris, all smiles, would present it to the husband for his breakfast.

The rest of the bread was made more methodically. Marta would shape the dough into flat circles, tossing them on top of one another into a waiting bowl. Then she would take the uncooked pita loaves out to the small stone oven and stand there, baking each one until they were all done. The husband would be long gone by this time, and so Marta would serve Idris and Adila their breakfast. Only after they had eaten would Marta break her fast for the day. Marta gobbled down not only her own breakfast, but any crumbs and scraps that had been discarded by the husband and his wives. She was desperate to nourish her body now that she was again surrounded by food.

Marta scrubbed the laundry by hand outside, then hung it up to dry. She chopped vegetables, and aired the bedding. And then the day's chores really began.

The husband sold a variety of goods at his stall in the market, but one of the most popular items was a certain wicker basket that Adila had devised years ago. The baskets had delicate geometric patterns in different colours of wicker on the outside and were prized for their beauty. But their real value lay in the fact that they were waterproof. Adila weaved them so tightly that once they were filled with water, the wicker reeds would expand slightly and block out all the holes. Women in the area loved these baskets because they were so light to carry to the well. Before Marta's arrival, Adila would make the baskets all afternoon, and Idris would sort out the wicker and decorate the outsides of the baskets. But after Marta came to live there, Idris would go up onto the roof and sulk or she would go the mosque or the baths. Marta assisted Adila in her place. The husband would come home and beat her, yelling "You lazy Armenian. An extra pair of hands, yet no more baskets." Idris would watch, a look of satisfaction on her face. Adila was afraid to say anything for fear that Marta would be turned out of the house.

Her only respite was donning a black chador and accompanying Adila to the market. The fine mesh that covered her face provided Marta with welcome anonymity. She walked freely beside Adila through the streets of Aintab. Moslem women had several advantages in the black robe and veil. A Moslem woman was a nonentity. Adila told her stories of women who travelled to their lovers unseen, and others who had carried secret messages and helped to overthrow the old government. It was because of the black robe and veil that Adila was able to say her prayers at the abandoned Armenian church each day. And it was because of the black robe that she had been able to save Marta.

But the black robe that provided so much safety was also a symbol of all that was wrong with a woman's place in this veiled world. It didn't take long for Marta to realize exactly what was expected of her as part of the "husband's" household. Now that she had entered his harem, it was the husband's right to ask anything of her. Marta's refusal would lead to another deportation — and she knew she wouldn't survive a second one.

Home

As the days blended into weeks, Marta's cheeks became less hollow and her figure began to fill out. Marta was not the only one to notice the change. There were angry whispered words between Idris and Adila, and Marta could hear her name mentioned in the fury. And it didn't help matters that the husband no longer complained of her presence.

The tension in the hut reached a peak by autumn. Idris was past jealousy. Now she was angered by her husband's continued interest in Marta. Adila too felt ignored. "I should never have brought you here."

Neither she nor Adila had any surviving children, and if Marta ever had a child, then she would automatically become first wife. This was something neither wife would risk.

Ironically, it was Idris who solved the problem.

"My youngest sister is about to have her first baby," Idris mentioned to Adila one day. "I am going to Marash to be with her, and I will not leave that girl in this house while I'm gone."

"Then you're taking her with you?" asked Adila.

Idris was so relieved to be finally rid of Marta that she had the driver take her to the orphanage gates first, before she went on to her sister's house. Marta could only imagine the beating she got when she returned home.

As soon as Marta was inside the orphanage complex she tore off the hood of her chador and breathed in freedom. This was the safest home she had ever known and it felt wonderful to be back, but she noticed that it was uncommonly quiet. She looked around, expecting to see children playing games in the courtyard, or missionaries walking briskly from one building to another. But the place was empty.

She walked up to the building that had been Miss Younger's office and knocked on the door. It took Marta a moment to realize that the woman who answered the door was Miss Younger. Gone was the neat bun of blonde hair, and in its place was dishevelled grey. Worry lined the woman's face, aging her by decades.

It took Miss Younger the same moment to realize exactly who it was standing at her doorstep. Marta had left the orphanage just a few short months ago, rosy-cheeked and dressed like a boy. Now she looked like a careworn Turkish housewife. But the eyes belonged to Marta.

Miss Younger wrapped her arms around her former

charge and hugged with surprising strength. "It's so good to see you," she cried.

Miss Younger knew better than to ask after the others who had been deported with Marta. The question would have been as painful as the answers. Instead, she thanked God for the one who came back. She ushered Marta into her office and made her sit down in the guest chair.

"Would you like to stay here?" asked Miss Younger.

"Yes."

"Our orphans are gone," said Miss Younger in a voice tinged with sadness. "Many were deported, and many were taken from here and put in Turkish orphanages. Soon, they won't even know that they were born Armenian."

Marta bent her head in sadness. "At least some will live."

The two women got up and walked through the empty streets of the orphanage complex. Marta could imagine flickers of images of orphans who had been and who would be again. They passed the courtyard where Marta had last seen her sister, and they passed the spot where Paris had died. On one side of the courtyard was the boys' orphanage where Kevork had lived, and on the other was where Marta and her sister Mariam had lived with all the other girls. Miss Younger and Marta walked side by side until they reached the building where all of the missionaries had been housed. "You may stay here with me," said Miss Younger. "You're no longer a child."

She led Marta to a small bedroom beside her own which had belonged to Aunt Anna. "Stay as long as you wish," she said. And then she went to her own room and fetched a long black western-style skirt and a white shirtwaist blouse. She laid the new clothing on the bed.

Marta looked down at the bed and the western-style clothing. Her own Turkish outfit was much more comfortable, although it would be a treat to sleep in a bed instead of on a mud floor. But this room was not right.

"I'd like to go back to my old bed," Marta said, picking up the shirtwaist and skirt and hugging them to her chest.

"But you'll be alone," said Miss Younger.

"I know."

She and Miss Younger shared a simple meal of olives and cheese and a few dried biscuits in an empty dining hall. As Marta looked down the long tables, she imagined the ghosts of so many orphans, sitting alongside of her. She imagined Kevork sitting there too, and her sister Mariam. Even the ghost of Aunt Anna was there, walking between the tables, making sure that everyone had enough to eat.

After dinner, Marta walked in the moonlight back to her old room. She was still wearing her

Turkish house clothes, although the chador had been abandoned. She set the shirtwaist and skirt on her bed. Perhaps tomorrow, she would put them on. She looked down the row of empty beds — all bare to the mattress — and walked over to the one where her sister had slept. Crouching in front of it, she lay her head down on the mattress and breathed in the faint scent of her sister. "Please be safe," she prayed.

Her own bed was also bereft of bedding and she was too tired to go back out and walk to the laundry at the other end of the complex for linens. Perhaps later, she said to herself, and then lay down on the bare mattress, dressed in her Turkish clothes, but with the skirt and blouse wrapped around her for warmth. Around her neck she still wore the pierced coin on a leather strap. As she settled into her nest of clothing, her hand wrapped around the coin, holding it to her heart.

As she drifted off to sleep, she could feel her consciousness rise, hovering somewhere just above her. She looked down at the sleeping figure below and sighed. She had come so far.

Then as she watched, the clothing that she wore and the clothing that covered her disintegrated and disappeared. The bed disappeared too, and then the room. She blinked and looked down again, and realized that she was now lying naked on that same sandy shore where her journey had begun.

She saw herself waken and stretch, then rise. She watched as Marta walked towards the glistening blue water. She stepped in, the cold wetness enveloping her feet with a shock. She looked down and marvelled at the seductive sensation of waterborne sand swirling around her toes and tickling at her ankles. But then the swirling turned into a tugging, and she felt herself being pulled down in an undertow. She was about to cry out when her head dipped below the surface.

In an attempt to free herself from the relentless pulling, she flailed her arms and legs. I want to live! She tried to cry out the words, but her mouth filled with brine.

Above her the water was no longer blue, but black, and the sand below her had given way to a tunnel. The inexorable pulling continued, and Marta tried to hold her breath, but then finally gave up and breathed in a huge gulp of salt water. With a shock, she realized that she could breathe the salt water as if it were air.

Just as she was becoming accustomed to the whooshing ride through the salty tunnel, it came to an end. Marta's feet touched solid ground and all the water swirling around her drained away. Marta found herself standing naked, save for the gold coin around her neck.

She heard a rustling sound behind her and turned. There stood an emaciated woman wrapped in a stiff white sheet. Marta's throat filled with tears when she regarded the woman's hollow eyes and sunken cheeks. This woman had suffered through famine and ravages too. Marta reached out to touch the woman's hand — to give comfort. Then she noticed the scars on the knuckles and the needle marks on her arms. With a start, she understood that this was Paula. Marta's heart was filled with sorrow.

"I want to live!" Paula cried.

Marta opened her arms to comfort the frail woman, and as she did so, she felt a strange tingling throughout her limbs and a prickly cold feeling at the back of her scalp. Paula opened her arms as if to return Marta's embrace, and Marta felt a loving warmth envelop her.

And then Marta no longer existed. She had just stepped inside of Paula.

Paula

An incredible fatigue enveloped Paula, and as much as she wanted to stay awake — to try and figure out what was happening to her — Paula realized that it was impossible for her to keep her eyes open. Her knees buckled beneath her and she collapsed into a dreamless sleep.

When she awoke, she found herself again lying in an unfamiliar bed. Her hand was still clutched around what she thought was the pierced coin, but when she looked down at it, she realized that it was a round adhesive disk stuck to her chest. What she thought was the leather strap was actually a wire, connecting the disk on her chest to a monitor at the side of her bed. She looked down at her body and recognized the blue material. Her sensibilities were rapidly returning to her, and she realized that she was dressed in a blue hospital robe, a starched white sheet stretched taut across her bony hips.

She lifted a hand to her face. It was not the tanned, capable hand that had been Marta's. It was the bony, damaged hand of Paula. There was a piece of white tape stuck onto the back of it, just above the angry scarred knuckle. It held in place a needle with clear plastic tubing from which a faintly yellow liquid coursed.

Paula recognized that liquid, and restrained her other hand from pulling the tubing out. Where once she would have considered the life-sustaining fluid an intrusion, now she struggled to be thankful for it. Her eyes followed the path of the plastic tubing and she saw that it was hooked up to a beeping book-sized monitor. She also noticed wires that were coming out of a video screen. With her unencumbered hand, she followed the path of the wires underneath the neck of her hospital gown to their end on her chest. There were a half a dozen or so of the wires attached to her skin with those round adhesive disks. They were monitoring her heart, Paula realized, as she watched the blips on the video screen with her hand placed over her heart.

The bed in which she lay was narrow and not well padded — it was little more than a stretcher. The jail-like sides were pulled up and Paula swallowed back her anxiety as she tried to convince herself that she had been put in this room for her own good. Her eyes darted nervously around, taking in the pseudo-cheery flowered wallpaper border, the yellow painted walls, and the soothing hums from all the monitors. She was the only person in the room, and it was quite small. She stared at the door, willing someone to come in, and finally, her wish came true. A woman in a pastel peach pantsuit with a stethoscope around her neck tapped gently on the door, and then entered, not waiting for permission.

The woman scanned the monitors and then she looked directly into Paula's eyes. "We thought we were going to lose you," she said.

"What happened?"

"Cardiac arrest."

Paula did not reply. What could she say? She knew she'd been given another chance.

Paula drifted into a long healing sleep and when she awoke she realized that she was no longer alone. Her mother, father, and brother were hovering over her, watching her every breath. Paula's heart leapt for joy at the sight of her family. When she had lived as Marta, the absence of the family had left her shrouded in an indefinable sadness. For all their faults, and in spite of all the angry words that had passed between them, Paula knew how fortunate she was to be part of a family. Her eyes locked on her brother Erik's. "I am so sorry," she said.

He looked at her with confusion. "Sorry for what?"

"Sorry for being such a rotten sister."

Erik's eyes teared up, and he angrily swiped at them with the back of his knuckle. "Don't be stupid."

Paula noticed that her mother, who was usually immaculately groomed, was wearing a wrinkled blouse and her hair was down. "We're so happy to have you back," she cried.

Paula's father said nothing. He simply held her unencumbered hand and squeezed it far too hard.

The nurse shooed them away after a few minutes. "Paula needs her rest," she said. Moments later, the same nurse brought in a tray and set it on Paula's lap.

Paula stared down at the selection on her tray and was surprised to have the same reaction as before. Eating was the enemy. She lifted her teaspoon and dipped it into the applesauce, coating the bowl of the spoon with a thin glaze. This she brought to her mouth and licked. As the minuscule portion of sustenance stuck at the back of her throat, Paula stifled an urge to gag. This is medicine, medicine,

medicine, she chanted. Then she stared at a blob of glistening red Jell-O, shivering in the middle of a chipped bowl. Through sheer force of will, Paula stuck her spoon into that and broke off a small spoonful. She placed it between her lips like a sacrament. This is medicine, medicine, medicine, she chanted. The gelatin dissolved with her saliva and she swallowed it down. She lay her head back against her pillow and closed her eyes in exhaustion. She could eat no more.

When she opened her eyes, Gramma Pauline was standing at the side of the bed, looking fragile with anxiety. She was not wearing her volunteer smock. Instead, she had one of her myriad of colourful silk tunics and flowing palazzo pants. With a shock, Paula recognized this outfit for what it was. It was almost identical to the Turkish house outfit she had worn in her days at the harem.

Gramma Pauline's white hair rippled free down her back and her jewelled fingers with their beautifully almond-shaped nails were intertwined with Paula's weak ones. Paula lifted her grandmother's hands up to her lips and kissed them, breathing in the heady aroma of turpentine and Dove soap.

Such close sight of the hands gave Paula another jolt. They were more than familiar. She looked up into her grandmother's face and was startled by a new sense of recognition. "Mariam?" she asked.

Pauline tipped her head to one side and regarded her granddaughter in confusion. "What did you call me?"

Paula flushed. The last thing she wanted to do was to upset her grandmother. How could she possibly explain what had happened to her? "You just reminded me of someone for a minute," she said evasively.

"My mother's name was Mariam," said Pauline.

Paula shook her head as if trying to clear out the cobwebs. "That's strange," she said. "I just had a dream that I had a sister named Mariam."

"Perhaps when you're feeling better, you can tell me about your dream," said Gramma Pauline.

"I would like that," said Paula. "In the meantime, could you buy me a notebook and pen? I want to write down as much of my dream as I can remember."

Pauline was taken aback by Paula's request. Her poor delicate grandchild was literally starving herself to death, and she'd just had a cardiac arrest, yet she wanted a notebook? She didn't argue, though. Whatever made Paula feel better had to be all right. "I'll get you one today," she said.

Paula's internist was a petite dark-skinned woman who would pop in on her at odd times during the day to check on the monitors. She seemed happy with what they told her. "I suspected that you had ventricle arrhythmia," the doctor said. "It happens in people who binge and purge."

The cold summation made Paula cringe. It shocked her to realize that her eating habits had caused so much harm to her body. And the irony was that she had always considered her dieting as part of a healthy lifestyle. "Will the damage be permanent?" she asked.

"I can't say just yet," the woman replied. "We'll observe you for forty-eight hours here in C.C.U. If you're still stable by then, you can go over to the medical ward where we'll get you walking around. We'll monitor your heart with a portable unit. If all is well at that point, you can go home."

The four days she spent in the hospital offered few moments when Paula was not being poked or prodded with needles, or encouraged to walk up and down the hallways with a cardiac monitor hung around her neck, making her feel like a horse with a feedbag. The rare snatches of solitude she could steal were taken up with writing down everything she could remember about her dream. She had a feverish need to get it written down, and even as the hours passed, she could feel the memories slipping away.

On the day she was to be discharged, Paula was sitting in the sun room at the end of the hallway, engrossed with the story she was writing in her notebook. Dr. Tavish walked into the room and quietly sat down beside her. She was so absorbed in her writing that her pen flew out of her hand in surprise when he greeted her.

"It's nice to see that you've found a new obsession," Dr. Tavish commented dryly as he retrieved the pen from the carpet and handed it to her.

If only it were so simple, thought Paula. It would be wonderful to have the freedom to abandon her problem with food as easily as she could put down her pen. The comment made her realize that people who hadn't been through an eating disorder really couldn't understand how powerful it was. She looked up at him and was gratified to see his familiar kind eyes and friendly smile. She placed the pen on top of the page and then closed her notebook.

"Thank you for coming," she said.

He nodded, "I am so sorry that it had to come to this."

"So am I."

Dr. Tavish didn't say anything for a moment. It was as if he were struggling with the words. Finally, he blurted out, "Paula, there's an opening at Homewood."

Paula looked at him, her eyes welling with tears, "I want to go home."

"But that's not the question right now. The question right now is, do you want to live?"

"Yes," she said fiercely. "I want to live."

"Then you'll need further treatment."

The Hunger

December 29, 111 pounds

Paula ultimately agreed with Doctor Tavish that Homewood offered her the best chance of survival, but her parents were reluctant to see her leave town to be treated in another city, especially so soon after almost losing her. After much soul-searching they finally decided that she would leave on January 3, meaning that Paula would still have a few days at home between leaving the Brantford General and her admission date at Homewood.

There were pitifully few personal possessions for Paula to take home with her from the Brantford General when she was discharged. Her mother had brought her an old pair of sweats and a T-shirt to change into, so aside from the clothing she arrived in, her duffel bag held nothing but her journal and pen.

Paula stepped into her living room. Her heart ached with homesickness. It would be so wonderful to be able to stay here amidst the familiar things and with her loving family, but she knew that the old routines would quickly set in and she would be no further ahead.

Her mother had prepared a homecoming meal for her, careful to incorporate things that she thought her daughter might want to eat. Instead of the old ploy of serving fattening foods, Emily was trying a different strategy. There was a tray of fresh-cut vegetables in the centre of the table, and another bowl of fruit salad.

Paula and Erik and their father all sat down at the kitchen table, and Emily placed bowls in front of each. "Home made chicken noodle soup," she said with satisfaction. "Eat as much or as little as you like."

Paula looked down at the steaming liquid in her bowl and watched as the globules of liquefied fat formed in circles on the top. She knew that they were trying hard not to pressure her to eat, but all the same, she could feel three sets of eyes anxiously watching.

She took a sip and repressed the urge to gag. As she swallowed it, she repeated the chant in her head, "This is medicine, medicine, medicine."

"It's good, Mom," she forced herself to say, and then was relieved when she saw the anxiety leave all three pairs of eyes.

Surprisingly, they didn't object when she asked go to her room once she had finished half a bowl of soup.

Paula was anxious not so much for the rest, but for the opportunity to continue writing as much of her dream as she could remember.

Opening the door to her room was a shock. She had completely forgotten that her parents had redecorated it during her initial stay at the hospital. Someone must have realized how upsetting this was to her, because her beloved posters had been retrieved. They now hung in close proximity to their original positions on the wall. But the offending cabbage rose wallpaper was still there, and the burnished wood of her dresser was still hidden under glossy white paint.

There was a light tap at her door and she turned around. There stood Erik. "I wish I could have fixed it better," he said.

"You did a great job."

"I have something else for you," he said. And then he gave her the framed oil that Gramma Pauline had painted so many lifetimes ago.

"Where did you find this?" she asked, holding it to her chest.

"It was stuck in the basement on a shelf," replied Erik. "I don't even know why they took it. Maybe they thought it didn't match or something."

He shifted back and forth from one foot to the other and then said, "I have something else for you." He took a small white pharmacy bag from his pocket and handed it to her.

She took it, and looked in, and was surprised to find a package of laxatives. "What's this for?"

"They shouldn't have gone through your drawers like that," he said. "I know you're not going to use them anymore, but that's not the point. They're yours and they shouldn't have taken them."

Tears welled up in Paula's throat. She hugged her brother. It embarrassed her to think that not too long ago she had gone through his things to get at his money to buy food. She was no better than her parents when it came right down to it.

"Thanks," she said.

"After you lie down for a bit, maybe we can play some *Civilization II* together?"

"Sure thing," she said.

And they did.

January 2, 111 pounds

Gramma Pauline came to visit on the day before she left for Homewood. There were so many things Paula wanted to ask her, but she didn't quite know where to start. Finally, she asked, "Gramma, where are your parents buried?"

Gramma Pauline hesitated before answering cryptically. "My parents who brought me to Canada are buried in Mount Hope Cemetery."

"Can you take me to see their graves?"

"I can take you now, if you'd like."

Mount Hope Cemetery was only a few minutes' drive from the house. When they got out of the car, Paula gripped her coat close to her and followed her grandmother through the rows of headstones. Pauline stopped in front of two matching small ones and bent her head in silent prayer.

Paula stood beside her, closing her eyes and

saying a prayer of her own. She was almost afraid to open her eyes and look down at what must be inscribed on the stones.

When she finally did look, she gave a small gasp of surprise.

One said:

Kevork Adomian b. 1900 d. 1967

The other said:

Marta Adomian b. 1902 d. 1968

So they did exist! They had both survived, found each other again, got married ... Her dream was a dream, but also reality. What she had lived through had actually happened.

Then another thought struck her. Pauline's mother wasn't Marta.

Paula turned to her grandmother in confusion. "I thought your mother's name was Mariam."

Pauline breathed a deep sigh. "My birth mother. Yes."

In silence they drove home.

Sunday January 3, 111 pounds

They presented her with a contract at Homewood. It stated that she agreed to stay for a minimum of six months, and that she agreed to participate in a "collaborative weight normalization treatment program consisting of ten phases." That meant that she would eat the food they gave her, and participate in the counselling sessions, the weighing sessions, the leisure sessions, and everything else that they suggested. She signed it.

There were seventeen other patients on the ward when Paula got there — sixteen young women and one teenaged male, and the first thing she noticed was that they were all thinner than she was. It made her feel huge.

Her room was small and L-shaped, and she shared it with Linda, who had been there for two weeks. A full-length mirror was attached to the wardrobe that separated the two halves of the room. Paula avoided gazing in as she walked past it to get to her bed. One good thing was that she had the window on her side of the room. Paula gazed out at the snow-covered trees and hoped and prayed that she would be able to leave by the time the blooms were full.

Paula had brought an overnight bag with her. It contained a few toiletries, some clothing, her journal, and the oil painting from Gramma Pauline. They had also asked her to bring either a bathing suit or short shorts and a crop top, so she had brought with her the shorts and top that she used for jogging. That first night, she slept with her hands on the painting under her pillow and cried herself to sleep. She dreamed that her hands were capable and strong and no longer scarred by her own teeth.

Monday, January 4, Phase 1

A small tap on the door roused both her and Linda early the next morning.

"Time for weigh-ins," sighed Linda, as she rolled onto her side and fell back asleep.

Paula sat up groggily on the side of the bed and watched as the door opened and a woman in a flowered smock and black stretch pants entered. Her name tag identified her as Candy. How ironic, thought Paula.

"Why don't you go first?" she suggested to Paula, gazing at her over the top of her glasses as she made a note in her clipboard.

She asked Paula to go to the bathroom, but left the door open a crack to make sure that she didn't have water — not even a sip — before the weigh-in. She handed Paula a hospital gown through the bathroom door, "You wear that, and nothing else," she called through the crack.

Paula walked down the hallway to the weigh-in room, feeling like a prisoner on the way to an execution. She hated being weighed by someone else. It was such a humiliating experience! It was the same kind of weigh scale that Dr. Tavish had a the clinic, and Paula stepped up onto it and automatically began to slide the weights to where they should be.

"We do it differently here, Paula," said Candy. "You've got to turn around so you can't see your weight."

Paula looked incredulously and the nurse. "Why should you know something about me that I don't know?"

"It's the rules, Paula. You signed the contract."

Humiliated, Paula turned around and listened as the weights slid into place. "How will I know if the program is working if you won't let me see what I weigh?"

"Focus on making yourself well, Paula. Leave the numbers to us."

After the weigh-in, Paula was allowed to go back to her room to get dressed for breakfast. She walked back down the corridor to the dining area and pulled up a chair next to Linda. She looked at all the girls sitting in their places and an image of the dining hall at the orphanage flashed through her mind.

Paula heard a screeching, rumbling sound coming from somewhere down the hallway. "It's the food truck," said Linda, a small shudder coursing through her body. It was an awful sound.

When it arrived, the food lady handed out carefully prepared individual trays, checking off names as she did so. The tray that she handed Paula contained two slices of toast with pats of butter, a boiled egg, a carton of milk, and a half grapefruit. "You don't expect me to eat all that, do you?" she asked.

"You must eat it all," said the food lady. "It's in your contract that you've agreed to follow the program here precisely."

Paula looked at the tray that Linda was given, it contained a bowl of raisin bran, milk, and an egg. "How come you've got less than me?" she asked.

"You learn what to order after awhile," whispered Linda in a quiet voice so the food lady couldn't hear. "Raisin bran counts for the carbs and the raisins in it count as the fruit. It saves you a whole lot of eating."

"Is that what you have every day?" asked Paula.

"You can't order it every day or they catch on, but I order it every other day."

The next humiliation was awaiting Paula after breakfast. She found out that in Phase 1, she was not to be trusted to be on her own for a full hour after every meal. She and Linda and two other girls played euchre to make the time pass.

Lunch and dinner routines were much like breakfast, and Paula felt that she was being stuffed like a Thanksgiving turkey. Each meal, she was forced to eat some variation of two starches, one protein, one fruit, and one milk. There was also the dreaded "high energy" food that had to be consumed once a day. Basically, that was one fattening dessert like a slice of cheesecake, a brownie, or cookies with milk. Paula noticed on the first day that most of the girls opted to take their high energy food during lunch. Linda explained to her later that night when they were in their room that the dessert selections at lunch were less brutal than those at dinner. "You can get away with a yogurt and fruit," she explained.

Weigh-ins were done on Mondays and Thursdays, and it was after her first Thursday weigh-in that Paula found out what the jogging shorts were for. "We'll be doing your first videotape this afternoon, Paula," announced Candy that morning after weigh-in.

Linda explained that she'd have a number of these done by the time she was through. Paula cringed at the idea of seeing herself in her revealing shorts and top. More humiliating was the thought of having a stranger videotape her in such vulnerable clothes. It was such an invasion of privacy. After the taping, Paula had been made to look at a chart of different body types and she was supposed to circle the body parts that most reminded her of her own. She angrily chose the fattest thighs and the fullest face and other terrible body parts

She and Candy sat and watched the video together later on. Paula was stunned at what she saw. The figure in the film was hunched over as if she were ashamed of herself. Was that really what she looked like? She also noticed the protruding collarbone. And her knees! They were made of huge knocking bones.

Every chance she got, Paula would curl up on her bed by the window and she would write in her journal. There were two parts to it now: one about her past life experiences, and one about the regimented life she was now living.

Monday, January 18, Phase 2

Two weeks of constant eating and constant supervision led to Paula's promotion to Phase 2. She was afraid of what that meant on the scales. She already knew what it meant on her body. When she looked at herself in the full-length mirror in her room, she fixated on her thighs and how much bigger they were getting. This was supposed to be healthy?

But the graduation in phases also meant that she had added privileges. Her activity time could now be spent in either the library or the chapel. Paula loved going to the chapel because it was almost always empty. The high-ceilinged room with windows all around and light streaming in had an airy freedom about it. On one wall was a poster showing the silhouette of a mother holding her newborn in front of an open window. There was a look of pure unconditional love in the mother's eyes. Paula would stare at the picture and she would go into a kind of trance. More than once, Candy came down to find her to let her know that it was time for yet more food.

Her parents and Erik came to Guelph once a week to see her, but visiting time was limited, and they never seemed to know what to say. Most of the half hour would be spent in silence.

Gramma Pauline also came down once a week. There was so much Paula wanted to ask her, but this wasn't the place. She knew that once she got onto the later phases of the program that she would be allowed to go off the hospital grounds for short visits. She looked forward to the day when she and her grandmother could go off somewhere private where they could talk.

Mandy came once. Paula hadn't been expecting her and she felt humiliated that her old friend would see her in such a vulnerable condition. "Forget it," said Mandy, hugging her. "It could just as easily be me here." Mandy brought with her a gigantic "get well" card that had been signed by most of the kids in Paula's home room. The thoughtful gesture brought tears to her eyes.

Monday, February 1, Phase 2

Linda graduated to Phase 3, just as Paula reached Phase 2. This meant that Linda only had to be supervised for half an hour after each meal. Paula and the others had to find someone else to make up their euchre fourth. The new fourth was a woman named Suzanne who was 250 pounds or more. She had been put on the ward after being diagnosed as a compulsive overeater. For the other girls on the ward, Suzanne was their worst nightmare. Would they end up looking like Suzanne if they continued eating all of this food?

Monday, February 15, Phase 2

A student nurse accompanied Candy on her weigh-in rounds. Paula didn't mind her watching as she went into the bathroom and changed into her gown. She didn't even complain when she followed close behind Candy, the two of them talking about her as if she couldn't hear. She refused, however, to let the student nurse observe while she got weighed. "I don't even know what I weigh anymore. Why should she?"

Paula was near to tears when she checked the board later that day to see if she had moved up a level. She hadn't. Again! Linda was already in phase 6. At the rate Paula was going, she felt that she would never get out of this place. She mentioned her concerns to Candy during a nutrition counselling session. "We'll add a calorie booster to your food," said Candy.

Paula had a sharp intake of breath. It seemed like such a sinister thing to do. Add calories to her food? She knew the calories of every bite she ate. How could she give up that control? "Let me think about it."

"It's not your decision, Paula," replied Candy. "If you're not gaining weight on the program, we've got to boost the calories. Your body's reached a plateau."

After that conversation, Paula looked at all of her dishes suspiciously. When a bottle of juice twisted open without giving that familiar vacuum "pop" Paula knew it had been tampered with. How many calories was she really consuming each day? It was terrifying not to have the numbers.

Monday, March 29, Phase 5.

When Paula scanned the postings after weigh-ins, she jumped for joy! Graduating to Phase 5 meant that she could have one unsupervised outing. She called her grandmother after breakfast.

"Would you like to take a walk in the park?"

"You did it!" Gramma cried. "Tell me when, and I'll be there."

She was allowed just thirty minutes off the hospital grounds, so Paula and her grandmother simply walked as far away from the hospital as they could in 15 minutes, then turned around and came back.

Paula began to ask her grandmother about her past before Georgetown. Pauline was still reluctant, but as Paula began to ask leading questions based on her dream, her grandmother began to open up. To her own surprise, she was pleased to have someone to talk to about the things that had happened in her own deep past. Paula's dream triggered her grandmother's memories and, together, they began to piece together the story of Grandma Pauline's history before coming to Canada.

June 28, Phase 5

It was taking longer than the contract said, and Paula still had not achieved her goal. More than once, she slipped back down a level and struggled to regain what she had achieved. It was so difficult for her to let go of the numbers, be they calories or pounds. Learning to trust was the most difficult challenge of all.

Linda had reached Phase ten over a month ago, but she often came back to visit her friends in Homewood.

It surprised Paula that she didn't consider Linda heavy, even though she obviously weighed so much more now. There was a sparkle in her eyes and a healthy glow in her cheeks. She exuded good health and happiness.

"Why are you out already, and I'm still here?" Paula moaned to her former roommate over a game of cards.

"Give yourself time," said Linda. "And give yourself credit for what you've already achieved."

That point was brought home to Paula later the same day when it was time to make one of the infamous video tapes. This time when she pulled on her jogging shorts, she noticed how snug they were. When she put on the skimpy top, she was alarmed by the bulges of fat under her arms. "That's not fat, Paula," Candy explained. "It's breast tissue."

When they sat down together to watch the tape, Candy announced, "I have a surprise for you. You can watch the segments you've done so far back to back."

And Paula watched the figure on the screen transform. What she noticed first was the posture. In the first shot, she was a hunched over waif with a protruding collarbone and knock knees. In the second shot, she was sitting up a little straighter. She also noticed that her collarbone looked better. By the third shot, she was sitting upright and there was a trace of a smile on her face. The knock knees were gone, but her thighs were way too fat. Paula looked back at the posture though, and then at the smile. It was okay.

The last picture showed a dramatic transformation. This was a woman who was comfortable in her own skin. She sat straight and proud and her eyes had a sparkle to them. Like Linda's. Her thighs were too fat though. And her stomach! "I have no angles!" she cried to Candy.

"You're softer, more womanly," replied Candy. "And remember, what you see as a rounded tummy will subside. When you first gain back the weight, it starts in your stomach and gradually gets redistributed."

Paula looked back at the face and the collarbone. And the hands. They were healthy and capable and strong. The stomach would subside, she told herself. This was progress, but it was terrifying.

July 5, Phase 6

Paula hooted for joy when she read the posting and saw that she had graduated to Phase 6. She had finally passed the halfway point in her treatment! It had taken her much longer to get this far than she had ever anticipated.

Phase 6 symbolized a turning point in the program too. Patients who achieved this level were allowed a single overnight stay off hospital grounds each week.

Paula longed to sleep in her own bed, and she longed to spend some time in her own home. Most of all, Paula looked forward to visiting her grandmother far from the prying eyes of Homewood.

Her parents and brother came to bring her home for her overnight stay. It was wonderful to see them and it was a miracle to be going home, even if for just a short while.

Saturday, July 10

Paula wasn't strong enough to jog to her grandmother's on that first Saturday of freedom, but she could walk briskly and feel the air whip through her hair and ripple down her strong arms and legs.

Pauline was sitting on her verandah swing, sketching in charcoal. When she saw Paula come up the street, she put down her sketch pad and ran over to her, then hugged her hard. "I've got something to show you."

She led her to a part of the house that Paula had never seen. There was a trap door just outside the kitchen and it led down a set of stone steps and into a low-ceilinged root cellar. It was so low that Paula had to crouch down to get through. On the dirt floor amidst the cobwebs and the mason jars, stood an ancient travel chest, covered with dust.

"Open it," said Pauline.

Paula knelt before it and brushed the dirt off the top and then raised the lid. It opened easily. Inside was a bundle of cloth.

"We'll take it upstairs for a better look," said Pauline.

They spread the bundle out on the kitchen table and Paula gasped with surprise. The outer layer of the bundle was made of black cloth. Within it lay the tiny sickle! It gleamed as if it were new.

Paula picked it up and ran her finger along the inner blade and watched as a bead of blood formed on her fingertip. "I never dreamed I'd see this again."

She set it gently down on the table and then picked up the coarse black cloth that had been wrapped around it. When she opened it, she realized that it was a chador just like the one that she used to wear.

"That belonged to my aunt — my adoptive mother, Marta."

Paula held it up to herself and saw that it was the right fit. She breathed in the familiar dusky scent and a shiver of recognition coursed through her. The next layer in the bundle was colourful silky cloth. When Paula unfolded that, she found that it was a harem outfit, but much finer than the sort she had worn.

"This belonged to my mother, Mariam," said Pauline. She and I both wore outfits like that before the missionaries rescued us.

"You were born in a harem?" asked Paula.

"Yes."

"What happened to Mariam?"

"My father hired mercenaries to get her back."

"You mean he kidnapped her back?"

"Or rescued her back. She and I had been taken back to the orphanage by the missionaries, but the orphanage was being attacked by Turks. He knew that, and knew she was in danger. They would have rescued me back too, but they couldn't find me."

"And so you were left."

"Yes. That part of my life had ended, but a new one had just begun."

the hunger resource list

Eating disorder help organization:

In Canada:

National Eating Disorder Information Centre
(NEDIC)
College Wing 1-211
200 Elizabeth Street
Toronto ON
M5G 2C4
(416)-340-4156

website: http://www.nedic.on.ca

In the U.S.A:

Eating Disorders Awareness and Prevention
Incorporated (EDAP)
603 Stewart Street, Suite 803
Seattle WA 98101
(206)382-3587
1-800-931-2237

website: http://members.aol.com/edapinc

Armenian genocide novels:

The Forty Days of Musa Dagh
by Franz Werfel
paperback, Caroll & Graf 1990
ISBN 0-88184-668-6

The Road from Home
by David Kherdian
paperback, Beech Tree 1995
ISBN 0-68814-425-X

Further information:

Armenian National Committee of Canada
3401, rue Olivar-Asselin
Montreal, Quebec H4J 1L5
(514) 334-1299

Armenian National Institute
122 C Street, NW, Suite 360
Washington, DC 20001
tel: (202) 383-9009

website: http://www.armenian-genocide.org

Near Death Experience, further reading:

Beyond The Light: What Isn't Being Said About Near-Death Experience
P.M.H. Atwater
Birch Lane Press, NY 1994
ISBN 1-55972-229-0

Dying to Live: Near-Death Experiences
Susan Blackmore
Prometheus Books, NY 1993
ISBN 0-87975-870-8

Further information:

International Association for Near-Death Studies, Inc.
PO Box 502
East Windsor Hill, CT. 06028-0502
(860) 644-5216

website: http://www.iands.org